# The Ecstasy of Pupusas

*Filled with Love*

By Stephen Rocco

*This book is a work of fiction. Any resemblance to actual events or persons, living or dead, is entirely coincidental.*

"The Ecstasy of Pupusas, Filled with Love," by Stephen Rocco. ISBN 978-1-63868-074-1.

Published 2022 by Virtualbookworm.com Publishing Inc., P.O. Box 9949, College Station, TX 77842, US. ©2022, Stephen Rocco. All rights reserved.

*To my late brother, Salvatore Rocco.*
*"The toughest kid in Everett."*

# Chapter 1: The Departure

A HUMAN LEAF FLOATED slowly from the highest Sequoia in a sea of Sequoia, startling Chelsea awake before she hit the ground. "Another nice dream ending badly," thought the still-sleepy Chelsea. From what she could remember, she was flitting from tree to tree one moment, and plummeting to the ground the next. As she pulled the covers from her bed, Chelsea looked down at her feet. "Even my toes are ugly," she thought. She hated her snow-white complexion sprinkled with freckles, even on her toes.

"No time for this dialogue today," thought Chelsea. She could not wait to tell Maria the good news. Maria Gomez was the family's El Salvadoran housekeeper, whom Chelsea considered her best friend. She quickly dressed and raced to Maria's Kingdom – the kitchen. Chelsea was met by her somber mother there, who typically glamorous even at this hour, said that she had bad news. "Maria has taken another job in another home closer to her own Boston home." Chelsea immediately felt dizzy as her eyes welled up. Incredulous, she asked, "How?" "Why?" Her mom hugged her as Chelsea's body went from joy to grief in seconds. Finally, Chelsea sobbed, "Does dad know about this?"

"Of course," answered her mom. "Maria called him this week and apologized that she could not give a two-week notice." "Where is Dad now?" demanded Chelsea. Her mom told her that he was at her brother Jon's basketball game and would be home for dinner. "Naturally," thought Chelsea.

Chelsea retreated to her bedroom and buried her head under the pillow. She was graduating in one month from Wellesley High School, class of 2005, and the person most responsible for that would not be with her. She could almost touch the features of her best friend, whom she first saw five years earlier. Stout, with beautiful thick brown hair, and matching skin, Maria's face radiated warmth. At 40-something she had a round face, broad nose, and curved mouth that seemed to radiate up to her ears when she smiled. That mouth smiled so often that she had crinkled laugh lines in the corner of each eye. In those five years,

Maria's short arms had enveloped Chelsea and squeezed out all of her high school troubles.

Half asleep, Chelsea remembered the first time she had seen Maria make pupusas. She remembered grabbing a seat near the stove, the better to study and admire Maria's artistry. Maria's fingers moved deftly from one ingredient to another, one pan or skillet to another, as she inquired about Chelsea's plans for the day while she prepared her corn dough with flour, butter, and oil. She knew instinctively when to add each ingredient— too early, and the pupusas would be too moist and the cheese would leak out; too late, and the dry pupusas would crumble in your hands.

When the dough felt right in her stout fingers, Maria carefully folded and refolded the dough. When the texture felt right, she twisted each one into hockey puck-like discs, one after another. Maria then added cheese, beans, and some sort of meat—today it was chorizo or sausage, her dad's favorite—to each disc. Like the aristocrats who folded and refolded their napkins at dinner, Maria refolded each pupusa into purse-like forms, each edge sealed so perfect that nothing oozed out of Maria's treats until it was tasted.

These jewels were then lightly fried in El Salvadoran oil that only Maria was able to find. Her puposas were so lightly fried that they tasted like perfect Spanish croissants.

Startled awake by the sound of the garage door opening, Chelsea ran downstairs to confront her dad. "How could you let Maria leave?" demanded Chelsea. "Wow, calm down, honey," said Dr. Ryan, which was how most people referred to him, given his stature as chief of orthopedics at Wellesley Hospital. "I could not stop her, Chelsea," said her dad. "She had a golden opportunity to work closer to her home, and to work fewer hours, too." Chelsea knew that the five days Maria had to make the twenty-mile trek from Boston to Wellesley was tough on her. She also knew that Maria wanted to spend more time with her husband Carlos, and her children— Roberto, age 15, and Alisa, age 12.

Dr. Ryan added that Maria's new job had to be decided quickly, and naturally he allowed her to leave without proper notice. "Maria knew you would be upset, Chelsea, but she said she will call you as soon as she gets settled." Chelsea's brother Jon broke in, "We will get another housekeeper, Chelsea, no big deal."

As usual, thought Chelsea, in Jon's entitled world, one person could easily be replaced by another.

That night, at a dinner of steak and vegetables cooked by her dad, since her mom rarely cooked, the family ate largely in silence. Chelsea could almost smell Maria's pupusas, yucca frita, or seafood ceviche. Sipping from her glass of wine, Chelsea's mom commented that they would have to hire another housekeeper. Tall and statuesque and in her mid-forties, Helene Ryan was a Sophia Loren lookalike, with a perfect olive complexion reflecting her Italian heritage. Always fashionable, her mom knew she was good-looking and always reminded Chelsea to try and look her best.

"I do have some good news," said Dr. Ryan. Tall, lean, and athletic, Dr. Ryan appeared older than his wife, although they were the same age. He was prematurely gray and wore glasses that gave him a distinguished image of competence. He'd passed his deep blue eyes and fair skin on to Chelsea. "I have been selected by the hospital to lead the merger between Wellesley and Boston Hospitals." "Oh great," said Helene. "There goes our trip to Italy."

"Please Helene, this promotion is a sign of respect." Respect was a common word in Dr. Ryan's vocabulary. He was proud that he was the first person in his working-class Irish family to go to college. He was revered in the community for both his compassionate bedside manner and his superb surgical skills. Even the many professional athletes whose careers he had saved referred to him only as Dr. Ryan. As Chelsea saw it, respect to her father meant status, money, and living in a big home in Wellesley.

Turning to Jon, Dr. Ryan praised his son, "That was a great shot you made." "Thanks, Dad, "said her brother. "The coach didn't even want me to take it." "What's wrong with your coach?" said Dr. Ryan. "He should know that you are the team's best shooter!" "He's a jerk," scowled Jon. Typical, Chelsea thought as she listened to this exchange between father and son – complaining like friends, instead of talking about something important like Maria.

Jon, age fifteen, a sophomore at Wellesley High School, was already a starter on the varsity basketball team. Everything came easy to him in Chelsea's opinion. He was smart and popular, plus he had inherited the good looks of his Mom. Already six feet tall, he possessed the physique of his dad but had his mom's dark hair, dark deep-set eyes, and a strong chin.

While Chelsea's high school years were marked by self-doubt and a need to "fit in" somewhere, Jon's were marked with confidence that everyone noticed – even her dad. While her dad was always on her in high school to improve her grades, his professional ceiling for her was to become a nurse. For Jon, however, Dr. Ryan talked about him following in his footsteps and becoming a doctor.

Even when Jon had a blemish in eighth grade involving a female classmate, he escaped any repercussions. Apparently, as Chelsea learned about the incident from others, Jon found out that a classmate was deathly afraid of dark, confined spaces. With the help of some male classmates, Jon engineered an escapade where the girl was locked in a school closet for the entire lunch period. Dr. Ryan blamed the "prank" on Jon's friends and never reprimanded him about it.

"Want to watch the Red Sox, Dad?" asked Jon after dinner. "Sure, bud, provided you finished your homework." "Of course," Jon replied as he left the room. Chelsea observed that her dad failed to congratulate her on her admission to her number one college choice. She had been admitted to a top nursing program at Southwynd College in upstate New York.

Helene poured another glass of wine as she and Chelsea sat in silence. Chelsea started to discuss Maria's sudden absence when Helene interrupted her to complain about her new job as a library aide. Her mom had not worked since her children had been born, and Dr. Ryan thought it would be good for her to be out of the house. Chelsea also thought her father encouraged the new job to save money as her mom's favorite pastime was buying clothes. She constantly lectured Chelsea about her appearance and her need to work out more. Chelsea naturally interpreted these comments as her mother thought her daughter was fat. "Now that you will be off to college, you will want to look your best," said Helene.

Chelsea knew instinctively that her mom did not want to talk about Maria any further because of Helene's distracted, almost absent gaze. Seeming to return to reality, she gazed at Chelsea and talked about her second favorite subject beyond clothes, and that was Chelsea's future. "Remember, don't you get married before you are thirty," said Helene. "Concentrate on your career and friends. You have plenty of time to have kids."

Feeling even more isolated without Maria's presence, Chelsea went upstairs and cried herself to sleep.

# Chapter 2: Old Soul

DRIFTING IN AND OUT OF SLEEP, Chelsea could hear Maria's Spanglish, combining El Salvadoran and English. Chelsea soon became "Bicha" and Jon "Bicho." Maria had a certain lilt to her voice that made you want to understand her and laugh over her need to be understood. She explained that Bicha was a female bug in her country. Certain Spanish slang might interrupt any conversation with her, such as "a dundo" for a dumb person, or "puchia," translated as "oh shoot," which was as close to anger as this amazing woman would get.

Maria was such a culinary artist that Helene had surrendered all attempts to cook when Maria was hired. Initially she was hired as a housekeeper three days per week, but when Dr. Ryan tasted her pupusas and cerviches, he increased her time to five days, and she became a Monday to Friday fixture at the house.

During the summer months, her full-time work required her to occasionally bring her daughter, Alisa, now age twelve, and her son Roberto, who was now Jon's age, fifteen. Chelsea recalled an incident when Jon and Roberto got into an altercation while playing soccer together. After that incident, Roberto never came back. Maria's husband, Carlos, whom Chelsea met only once, worked as a painter. He seemed as quiet as Maria was effusive, and he spoke little English.

Chelsea recalled those summer days when Alisa would beg her to go to the nearby playground. She never had to beg hard, because Chelsea loved those visits as much as Alisa. A miniature version of Maria, with huge, almond-shaped eyes and glorious curls in her raven hair, Alisa radiated innocence. On the way to the playground, Alisa would pepper Chelsea with questions: "Why do you have so many clothes?" "How come your bedroom is so big?" "What is high school like?" Chelsea was so happy to be around children. Their innocence and curiosity made her feel special and relaxed.

From her conversations with Maria, Chelsea knew that Alisa shared a bedroom with her brother. The family shared a Boston apartment with Maria's brother Ramon, and they were trying to save enough to get their own apartment. She also knew that Alisa loved the playground because she was not able to play at the

one near her home. Maria and Carlos had seen hypodermic needles near the swings on one visit.

Chelsea's emotions that night ranged from anger to guilt over Maria; anger that Maria could leave her, and guilt that Maria's actions were done only because she was trying to give Alisa and Roberto the same things that Chelsea had.

In the weeks that followed, entering the spring of her senior year, Chelsea rationalized that at least she would be away at college next year. She had time to reminisce about her high school years and Maria's influence on that journey.

Early in her eighth-grade year, Dr. Ryan, over dinner, proposed that if Chelsea's grades did not get better, he might send her to a private high school. He even suggested that she live there. Chelsea, terrified at this idea, promised her dad she would work harder. Later that day, Chelsea complained to Maria that her dad treated her differently than her brother.

Wrapping her large arms around Chelsea, Maria reassured her, "Bisha, Dr. Ryan only wants the best for you."

Her dad, with her mother's blessing, also coordinated her attendance at the public high school with extracurricular activities. In addition to playing soccer, Chelsea joined the school band, where she played clarinet.

High school had also meant the loss of her best friend, Lucille, who hated her name so much she insisted that everyone call her "Lou." Pint-sized teammates in youth soccer, she and Lou were inseparable throughout middle school. A superb athlete in soccer and basketball, Lou literally had town coaches fighting over recruiting her for their youth teams. Unlike Chelsea, whom coaches had to remind to play harder or faster, Lou had an aggressive edge. She was also pretty and popular, unlike Chelsea, and feisty enough to yell at coaches on occasion.

The change in their relationship coincided with Lou's parents' separation the summer before freshman year. She recalled a ride to soccer practice that summer with Lou's dad that was largely silent. Her father's only question was to ask if Lou's

Mom was seeing anybody. When they got to practice, Chelsea watched as Lou's dad gave her a quick kiss and handed an envelope to Lou. "Give this to your mom, or she will take me back to court."

Chelsea's mom picked the girls up after practice. Lou was noncommittal about going to a movie that weekend, and in fact saw Chelsea less and less that summer. Chelsea recalled asking her mom that day if Lou's parents' divorce could be affecting Lou. Helene absentmindedly murmured that people sometimes had to make tough decisions.

That summer, over one of Maria's chicken pupusas, Chelsea shared with Maria how nervous she was about entering high school. Maria's eyes glistened as she revealed how nervous she had been when leaving her own country. "You will be fine, bicha, because you have an old el alma."

Curious, Chelsea asked what that term meant in English. In broken English, Maria said, "An old soul." She explained in a painstaking translation that in her village people believed that one was born with either an old soul or a new soul. From what Chelsea could understand, old souls have lived before and have a certain wisdom and affection for people. They instinctively know what is important in life. New souls experience everything for the first time and take time to acquire this knowledge. When Chelsea asked what kind of soul her brother Jon had, Maria quickly said, "New soul."

It was the Monday before school for her freshman year, and Chelsea, as usual, was chatting with Maria as she did her laundry chores. "I'm really scared about tomorrow, Maria. The school is so big." Maria laughed one of her big belly laughs and hugged Chelsea. "You will be fine. You have a mucha heart."

"Have you ever been scared, Maria?" For once, Maria grew misty-eyed and said," Yes, bicha. Mucha scared when I had to leave my country." "Why did you have to leave El Salvador, Maria?"

"I never wanted to leave my beautiful country. I lived in a small farming village called Arcatao, high up in the mountains. My father grew sugar, coffee, and white corn with the help of my brothers, Luis and Ramon. I was the baby and my job was to care for the chickens. My brothers called me the chicken girl. We all enjoyed our life in the mountains. I never wanted to leave, bicha. I had a happy life."

Maria told Chelsea how much she loved school and didn't mind the three-mile walk she made each day with her village friends. In the summer months after chores, they played in the river, although Maria laughed and said she always feared the water.

Nights, she would watch her mother cook as the men came in from the fields. The family loved to laugh and sing with her brothers, who played guitar. Maria seemed to be at that table singing as she looked away from Chelsea.

"Then why did you have to leave, Maria?" Maria sighed, "Someday I will tell you, bicha, but now you'd better get ready for soccer practice."

That night Chelsea googled El Salvador's political history. She quickly saw that the country was historically ruled by a dictator, who would last until another despot succeeded him. Chelsea read that this pattern changed in 1979 when the military, or "Junta," took over the government, deposing its president, Carlos Romero. Chelsea calculated that Maria would have been about her age then. Over the next thirteen years, until a United Nations-supported peace agreement was reached in 1992, the country became increasingly violent. The Junta battled peasants, farmers, even the college educated, whom they labeled "communista." Another divergent group opposed to military rule organized, and became known as FMLN. Chelsea read about the unbelievable violence that evolved with both groups. An estimated 75,000 people died in this civil war. Chelsea was aghast to read about the murders and rapes. No one was safe, including priests and nuns. Massive graves containing one thousand women and children were uncovered near the border of Honduras, close to where Maria lived.

Chelsea googled maps and eventually found Maria's village of Arcateo, located in northwest El Salvador in the Sierra Mountain range, close to the Honduras border. Chelsea read that as the civil war escalated, rebel groups who committed atrocities retreated to Honduras to escape. Chelsea vowed that at the right time, she would ask Maria how she managed to escape this violence and come to the United States.

That night, as Chelsea prepared for the first day of high school, she felt guilty as she compared her anxiety to any that Maria had suffered. " If Maria could overcome her troubles, mine are nothing in comparison," she thought as she fell fast asleep.

# Chapter 3: High School Troubles

THE MORNING AFTER the bad news of Maria's departure, Chelsea looked down at her acceptance to Southwynd College. I haven't even had the chance to show this to Maria, thought Chelsea. Given her dramatic journey through high school, Chelsea attributed her acceptance largely to Maria's influence.

Chelsea remembered those first freshman days at the high school. Unsure where to sit at lunch, she was happy to recognize Cassie, a friend from soccer captains' practice. They had bonded at the pre-high school practices because each was quiet and not considered a "star" player. Cassie laughed in agreement with Chelsea that they would probably have "retired" from soccer if not for their dads.

Cassie also played in the school band. Chelsea played the clarinet, while Cassie had chosen the saxophone, keeping a promise to her dad. The girls saw a lot of each other as a result. Cassie normally had lunch with her brother Taylor, who was a sophomore, so their lunch group consisted of freshmen and sophomores.

Occasionally at lunch, Chelsea — and frankly, all the lunch students — watched the large table where her friend Lou sat. This loud group of about ten students called attention to themselves with loud ruckuses, such as bread fights. School monitors often had to discipline this group, who did not seem to care what anyone thought of them. Lou seemed to fit right in with her new friends and even adopted their dramatic "goth-like" clothes. While Chelsea and her new friends laughed at these students, secretly she looked at them with a weird form of revulsion and fascination. Whatever they had, she thought, it had attracted her best friend Lou.

Chelsea had basically given up calling Lou that freshman year, because she was always busy. They talked briefly between classes when they passed each other in the halls. Lou asked her one day how soccer tryouts were going. Chelsea had even surprised herself by making the freshman team, and Lou seemed happy for her. Surprisingly, even to the coaches who called her personally, Lou decided not to try out for the team. Chelsea missed her best friend's alpha personality both on and off the field.

That fall of freshman year, Lou invited Chelsea to a party. However, it was during the time she was a member of the school band. Since the band had to play and march each Friday night for the high school football games, Chelsea declined the invitation.

Over that first year, academics, sports, and band kept Chelsea busy. Her grades, mostly B's with an occasional A or C, fortunately kept her father's attention on Jon. She and Cassie mostly played late in the soccer games, when the game was either won or lost. She could hear echoes of her coaches telling her in practice to be "quicker to the ball." Naturally, Chelsea interpreted this as "I'm average in everything." Over pupusas, Maria would convince Chelsea that she was special. "You will do something special, bicha."

That first year, Cassie's brother Taylor patiently helped Chelsea learn the clarinet. He was a first clarinet in the band and often played solos during performances. Tall and lanky, Taylor was a Bill Walton lookalike with burnt red hair, and freckles like Chelsea's. He was funny and quietly confident. Chelsea admired his confidence. When his friends made fun of Lou and her friends one day, he defended them and said, "They are okay." Occasionally Cassie and Chelsea found Taylor joining them at Saturday night movies that freshman year. By that spring, Chelsea could see that Taylor was interested in her. She was surprised and happy when he asked her to go to the movies only with him.

By the summer of 2002, before sophomore year, she and Taylor were officially dating. Taylor aspired to be an engineer and often told Chelsea how important junior year's grades were. He seemed older than other students his age, thought Chelsea. She was surprised when he said he might have to quit band next year. "I have to get into a good engineering school," explained Taylor, "and junior year's grades are crucial."

One summer night, Taylor was invited to Chelsea's parents for dinner. Maria prepared special empanadas for her guest. They were delicious, but her spicy sauces turned Taylor's white skin almost crimson. "I'm sorry, bicho," laughed Maria, "Take some agua."

Predictably, after Taylor left, her father complimented him. "He seems like a serious young man, Chelsea, who knows what he wants." As predictably, her mother cautioned her daughter not to get "too serious."

Privately her mother had offered to get Chelsea contraceptives if she was considering having sex. Embarrassed and shocked, Chelsea told her mother that was not necessary at all! In reality, Chelsea was happy that Taylor did not go further than heavy petting and had not put any pressure on her.

Chelsea's friend Lou had not played any sports that first year, neither basketball nor softball, in which she excelled. She began dating Nick, a sort of ringleader of her outlier lunch group. Two years older than Lou, Nick and she were seen around town riding on his new motorcycle.

By sophomore year, Chelsea felt much more comfortable in her school environment. Busy with her new friends from junior varsity soccer and band, she regularly had plans on nights and weekends. While she was still close to Maria, those intimate conversations with Maria over pupusas occurred less often. But Maria always had her broad smile and hug ready for her bicha, and she seemed happy for Chelsea.

Jon, an eighth-grader, was also making a name for himself in the town. His athletic skills had drawn the attention of his awaiting high school coaches in baseball and basketball. Dr. Ryan thought Jon had a chance to play varsity sports as a freshman, which was very unusual for someone his age. His brooding good looks had also captured the attention of Chelsea's girlfriends, who found him very attractive.

Early in Chelsea's junior year, things changed with Taylor. He had quit the band to concentrate on his grades but was still having problems with calculus. He said that they might have to see each other less often so that he could study. It was during this conversation that Chelsea started having second thoughts about Taylor. While they were discussing grades in general, Taylor said that maybe Chelsea should aspire for better grades. He explained that he thought she was very smart, and maybe being a nurse should not be her ceiling.

Chelsea did not hear the part about the ceiling. What she heard was that she was not good enough, and perhaps even lazy. Chelsea thought that Taylor reminded her of her father in this moment. In the following weeks, she could not get the image of authoritarian Taylor telling her what to do out of her mind. Taylor seemed to understand this, repeatedly calling her to apologize.

One morning, Chelsea shared her feelings with Maria. "Everyone does mistakes, bicha," observed Maria. While somewhere in her mind she knew Maria was right, Chelsea felt a hurt she didn't fully understand. All she knew was that she could not see Taylor right now. Eventually she stopped answering her cell phone whenever she saw his number light up.

It was during this period in January of junior year that she bumped into Lou in the school hallway. Sporting a new nose ring and purple hair, Lou asked if Chelsea wanted to go to a party that weekend. Unable to give the excuse of the band, Chelsea reluctantly agreed to go.

The night of the party, Chelsea put on many outfits and asked Maria to judge them. Maria loved all of them. "You always look beautiful, bicha," complimented Maria. Chelsea knew "nice" clothes probably did not make it with this group. Eventually she settled on a black lace vest and torn dungarees, which she accentuated with more tears she made with scissors.

The party was unlike anything Chelsea had ever seen. Nearly every one of the forty people at the house smoked pot. Many were running in and out of the bedrooms. The music was extremely loud and raw, and most of the kids were also drinking alcohol.

Lou rested largely on the shoulder of Nick throughout the night. Each seemed to be eyeing Chelsea, ascertaining whether she could be included in this group. Nick in particular seemed to instinctively know of Chelsea's insecurities, at one point making a comment about a "doctor's nice daughter." Lou seemed anxious to know what Chelsea thought of her friends.

Chelsea was simultaneously scared and intrigued by these people. She envied Nick and his friends' confidence and "to hell with it" attitude. But she was scared of their habits – sex and alcohol were a prominent part of this lifestyle.

The night flew by quickly, and gradually Chelsea became a bit more comfortable with the scene. She even ragged a bit on teachers that this group detested as being "uncool." However, she refused their attempts to coax her into drinking a beer or smoking a joint.

The next week, Lou called her at home inviting her to another house party that weekend. She was happy to be reuniting with Lou, and she had to admit she was reluctantly becoming enticed by this lifestyle. She loved being free from her day of worries, even if only for one night.

More house parties emerged in the cold winter months, sometimes occurring on both Friday and Saturday. Chelsea felt pressure to fit in and began to start drinking beer and smoking pot. While some people at these parties snorted cocaine, she drew the line there.

One night in February, she found herself dancing—and eventually making out with—Nick's best friend, Matt. Soon after that the four friends, Chelsea, Matt, Nick and Lou, would see each other during the weekdays. Normally they would drive around in Matt's car, drinking and smoking.

Maria noticed a change in Chelsea. "How are you, bicha?" Maria would ask as Chelsea answered, "I'm good, Maria," and run out of the house to join her new friends.

Spring schoolwork junior year naturally took a back seat to her new lifestyle. When her third-quarter grades came out, former B's were now C's, and her science grade became a D. Her father was very upset with her. "You are not going to become a nurse with a "D" in science," he warned. He threatened that a transfer to private school was still not out of the question. Chelsea just ignored his threats.

The partying continued through spring. Matt, the opposite of Taylor in every respect, was of Greek heritage, with dark curly hair and an athletic build. He hated school and wanted to open his own restaurant one day. Chelsea became more and more enamored with him. Matt began pressuring her to have sex with him, as Chelsea knew that Lou and the other girls in the group had sex with their boyfriends. Chelsea resisted crossing this mental threshold, however, until Matt basically warned that they were done unless she had sex with him.

Chelsea remembered the day when she hesitantly approached her mom about the offer she had once made about contraceptives. Surprisingly, her mother was almost businesslike when she got Chelsea's gynecologist to prescribe them. Helene did not even ask about why Chelsea wanted them or with whom she was making this decision. Helene just seemed relieved that her daughter would not get pregnant.

That April, Chelsea got ready for a big party at one of her friend's housees, and Lou was excited because the parents were going to be away for the whole weekend. Chelsea thought this might be the right time to have sex with Matt.

That night, perhaps because of the gravity of her decision, Chelsea drank more than usual. Usually, she drank only beer, but this night she drank vodka shots. Chelsea felt herself getting more and more removed from reality as she closed her eyes on the couch with Matt. The last thing she remembered while lying there was a nauseous feeling in her stomach.

# Chapter 4: The Journey

THE MORNING AFTER THIS WILD PARTY, Chelsea awoke in her own bed, unsure of how she had gotten home. The last she remembered, she was sitting with Lou, Matt, and Nick. At that moment, she heard her parents arguing downstairs. Her mother was almost hysterically yelling that they had to call the police. Suddenly, she heard a tap on her door, and when the door opened she saw the smiling face of Maria carrying Chelsea's breakfast: huevos rancheros – beans and eggs on a corn tortilla. Her churning stomach needed just this type of comfort food to pacify it.

Maria watched her inhale this treasure and told her that her parents were waiting for her downstairs. Chelsea asked Maria if she knew how she had gotten home. Maria shook her head, but she struggled to say Chelsea had been "enfermo," or sick, and that her clothes were soiled with "vomites."

Chelsea showered and then went down to meet her parents. Her father was pacing in the living room, which was abnormal, as he always seemed in control. Her mother was sobbing. They demanded that Chelsea tell them everything that had happened the night before. Chelsea explained that she had been at a party with Lou and drank too much alcohol. The last she remembered she was on the couch watching people dance and must have passed out. "Oh great", said her mom, "They could have done anything to you."

"You embarrassed this family and yourself, "said Dr. Ryan sternly. "Do you know how I got home?" asked Chelsea, as she felt her face burning and her eyes moisten. Her father said, "We are trying to figure that out. At 11 p.m. the doorbell rang and there you were—alone, and reeking of vomit." Chelsea turned to her mother and cried, "I'm sure nothing happened, Ma, because I did not get to the party until 9 p.m." Helene retorted angrily, " I don't care. I want to call the police on these people. They should not be having unsupervised parties."

Dr. Ryan sat down on the couch, and his face met Chelsea – blue eyes to blue eyes. "I want you to call Lou right now and demand that she tell you what happened." On speakerphone, while Chelsea and her parents listened, Lou assured Chelsea that her last memory of the party was accurate. "One minute you were on the couch talking to us, and the next minute you were vomiting all over everything.

Nick and I were not sure what to do, so we took you to your house, rang the bell, and quickly left." Reassured that Chelsea had not been violated, Dr. Ryan turned to his wife and said, "The police do not have to be involved." He then told Chelsea that she had disappointed the family, and she was grounded every weekend indefinitely. "You will stop seeing Lou now!" he commanded. "Now, go to your room until dinner."

Lying in bed, Chelsea blamed herself for causing her parents to be so upset. She questioned herself about why she wanted to hang around with Lou and these new friends. "Was it the excitement?" "Did I just want to reconnect with Lou?" "Why did I reject Taylor, who was like me, to associate with people who were not like me?" These issues were turning in her head when she heard a light knock at the door. It was Maria.

"How's my bicha?" she inquired as she enveloped Chelsea in a hug. "How could I be so stupid, Maria?" Chelsea asked. "Life is very hard sometimes, bicha, and sometimes we make mistakes that we cannot correct. My poor brother Luis got so 'loco,' bicha, from the 'troubles' in my country, he 'drink' himself to death."

"What happened to him, Maria?" asked Chelsea.

Maria sighed and answered, "I tell the whole story for you, Chelsea. You know how happy I was in my country, bicha, with my parents and brothers Ramon and Luis."

 "Around 1992 when I was about fifteen, my brothers came in from the fields very upset. They told us that soldiers had approached them and demanded that they join the military by the next week. Ramon said they were given rifles and told to practice using them. They would be expected to arrest people. Ramon knew that several of his friends had disappeared in the last months, after having been arrested and accused of being communists.

"My mother cried and sobbed, saying that her 'familia is la muerte'. (family is murdered or ended) My father wrung his hands in silence. Then my brother Ramon spoke up. "I have a plan," he said. Although younger than Luis, he was always the more vocal and confident one.

"I know someone who is a coyote, someone we pay to get us into America through Mexico. I have been in touch with our cousins in Boston, and they will help us get jobs. I will go first, then save money and send for Luis, and then you, Maria, and our parents." We found out the coyote would cost $3000 American money, and we had only $2000. My papa went into his bedroom and came out with $1000, his savings that he had been putting away to buy a bigger farm.

"Ramon left several days later with the help of the coyote. After a month, Ramon mailed a letter from Boston with his first check for Luis's trip to America. While he was waiting for the full amount, Luis, my 'triste' (sad) brother, was forced to fight with the Federales. Each night he would come home in tears and tell us that he and the others had to hurt the innocent. Never one to be a 'borrach' (drinker), bicha, Luis drank every night to ease his pain. He would whimper that he had hurt the ninos (children) and continue to drink more and more.

"When Ramon's payments were almost enough to pay for the coyotes, Luis suddenly disappeared. My distraught parents went to the Federales, who said he was with the Communists. Some in our village who were part of the FLAN said they did not know where Luis was." Chelsea became aware of Maria's tears, as she explained that the family never knew what had happened to Luis. "This was the end of my parents, bicha, because each died of a broken heart within two years. They searched for my brother until they died."

"My brother Ramon then let me know that I must leave for America immediately, as soon as I get the final payment. I was told to contact the coyote named Pedro. Pedro said that I must bring only two sets of clothes, the $3000 payment, and all the money I could get for the 'Ladrones' (thieves) that I might meet on the 1500-mile journey. I had only three hundred more American dollars.

"The day came when I was to leave. I met with Pedro and another coyote, Roberto. There were eleven other people, including a one-year-old baby and her parents who would go on the journey with us. I was happy to see that one of those going was a classmate from my school, Graciela. There were two vans, and as Pedro separated us, he directed Graciela into the other van. In my van were the baby and her parents, a young man about my age, and an older man like my father.

"Pedro collected the $3000 from each of us and explained how we would get to America. We were to drive through Guatemala into the town of Legheria in Mexico. Then we would drive to Juarez, where Pedro would have rafts for us to cross the Rio Grande into the United States, where more vans would be waiting to take us into the city of El Paso, Texas. My brother Ramon had told me that he would meet me in El Paso. I was so afraid of crossing the river. I am not a good swimmer, bicha. But Pedro, he laughed at me and said it was safe, and he had never 'lost' anyone.

"The trip took nearly two weeks through rugged terrain. We had lots of time to become friends with each other, all of us who simply wanted a better life. The young parents had a beautiful daughter, Ariza. Unlike my brother, Luis, Ariza's father Jose had fought with the rebels after the military destroyed his farm. He started to see the FLAN doing things that the military was doing in El Salvador – killing innocent people. Some military families' homes were bombed, killing innocent mothers and children. His young wife Lucinda agreed with her husband. She told me no one is safe in El Salvador. The older gentleman, Sal, had lost his farm to the 'Federales' and hoped to live with his sister in Texas.

"The man who was about my age, Carlos, sat next to me for the long ride. He was a fisherman who lived near the Pacific coast in San Salvador, in southeast El Salvador. He reminded me of my father — quiet, with dark features and a sturdy build. We enjoyed talking and laughing together, and I promised him one of my pupusas one day. He promised to help me cross the river in return. He told me he was going to New Orleans to work on a shrimp boat.

"The vans slowly made their way through the hills and deserts of Guatemala into Lecheria in Mexico. Pedro was a good coyote and provided us with water and food. Several times during the trip, we were stopped by masked men with guns. Carlos whispered to me that they were thieves who often robbed the people who traveled this journey. He explained that it was Pedro's job to negotiate with them. But one time, Pedro was not able to work things out. In Lecheria when we crossed into Mexico, our van was stopped by two 'policio.' They were large, thick officers, wearing sunglasses and wide-brimmed hats. We were ordered out of the van and told we would be arrested for illegal entry. After a brief talk with Pedro, the policio seemed to sneer as they said they would accept $400 from the five passengers. "We will let the baby go for free."

"Some of the passengers took off their shoes and socks, where they had hidden their money. All the money was collected, but I did not have enough for my share. One of the officers said, "That's okay, honey, you can come with us and we will work out payment." They were about to arrest me when Carlos ran to us with $100. "It will cost you $200 now," said the policio. Carlos gave him the other $100. I was so thankful to Carlos. I hugged him and told him that my brother would repay him. Carlos just smiled.

"Finally, the van got to the Rio Grande. Pedro told us that we would have to stay on the banks until night, when it would be easier to slip through. Pedro left, and when he came back he had what looked like play rafts that you see at the beach. I watched the river and shook with fear. The water did not look deep, but I could see a strong current. Then Carlos squeezed my hand and said, "Don't' be afraid. I am used to the sea."

"In the early morning hours, Pedro told everyone to undress. "I will have clothes on the other side. The water is not deep, but the current is quite strong tonight. You should hold on to the raft next to you and kick your feet. We must keep all the rafts together."

We all did what Pedro said, and all seemed okay until a short distance from the other side. One of the rafts got loose, and then all the rafts started turning over. Carlos grabbed me and pushed me onto the shore.

"Soon we heard Jose shouting, "My wife!" Jose was holding his daughter, but Lucinda was nowhere to be seen. Pedro raced down the river to try to find Lucinda. Pedro's assistant was waiting with dry clothes for us on the other side. He told us to stay quiet and dress quickly. I felt so afraid and sad for Lucinda as I dressed. Then we had to leave. I remember seeing poor Jose crying on the riverbank as he held his little daughter Ariza. We were all rushed into the waiting van. I never knew what happened to Lucinda, bicha, and I dream about her often.

"Finally, we came to the hotel where Ramon was waiting. My brother and I hugged as we both cried for joy and sadness. Carlos decided he would go with us to Boston, and we have been together ever since."

Chelsea cried as Maria revealed this incredible journey at a time when she was feeling sorry for herself. They embraced, and Maria whispered in her ear, "That old soul of yours has a lot of good to do." That day Chelsea made up her mind to use her talents, whatever they were, to the best of her ability. Chelsea said to herself that if someone as amazing as

Maria believed in her, she would have to learn to love herself.

# Chapter 5: Forever Changed

CHELSEA PUT THE FINAL TOUCHES of eyeliner on her best feature – her big blue eyes – and whispered to herself, "I made it." " It" being her graduation later tonight among the class of 2005 from Wellesley High School. She realized that this improved vision of herself began from within. For from that terrible night last year when she was left at the doorstep, covered in vomit, Chelsea made a determined effort at self-discovery.

Even though she had not heard from Maria since her departure, Chelsea felt her friend's presence and support. Chelsea had come to believe that Maria might be right about her. Perhaps she did have an old soul, and possessed certain gifts to be shared with the world. Chelsea's gifts might combine a love of children with a career predetermined by her dad – a pediatric nurse, maybe in an oncology unit for children.

From the day after that incident, Chelsea made a conscious effort to make some personal changes. To Lou, she was polite but firm that her days of partying were over. Chelsea avoided Lou's crowd during school lunch and often ate alone in those first weeks. When later Chelsea learned that Lou had dropped out of school, she chose not to reach out to her friend; a decision she grew to regret. Although in the past Chelsea had never really applied herself, she worked extremely hard that final quarter of her junior year. She even surprised herself by making the honor roll. Chelsea forced herself to read the great classics of Shakespeare and Hemingway, and she grew to appreciate the love of learning. Her college application essay touched on the beginning of her "lost" junior year and the dramatic change of self-discovery.

Chelsea rejoined the school band her senior year. She found out that her classmate, Emma, was dating Taylor, who was now a freshman engineering student at a local college. Taylor would meet Emma after band practice. At first Chelsea felt a tinge of regret seeing him. But his "no hard feelings" demeanor around her eased that wound. She was genuinely happy for him.

Her improvements also translated to the athletic field. She dedicated herself to having a "great" senior year. She led captain's practices for underclassmen and got herself into better physical shape. She jogged several times per week and started weight training. These improvements did not go unnoticed by her coaches. She was named one of the captains for senior year. Chelsea realized she was never going to be an athletic star like her brother, but she had a solid season for the team. Her parents also noticed her renewed commitment to the team and attended many of her games, often with Jon.

Chelsea was finally part of the sports conversation at the dinner table. In fact, just prior to Maria's abrupt departure, the family's mood had never been better. Chelsea made a concerted effort to bring happiness to the dinner table, a contentment that had often been absent. Despite the fact that they never really fought, her parents often seemed distracted and aloof toward each other. They seemed to communicate only through their children, rather than with one another. That spring, the aloofness eased.

Chelsea began to enjoy cooking more and more. She would shoo Maria out of the kitchen, and prepare meals for the family herself. Dr. Ryan particularly loved her seafood cerviche, and after this satisfying meal, he would relax and discuss how the merger was going at the hospital. Her mom expressed her interest in going back to school, a plan which her dad supported "one hundred percent." "What would you like to study, Mom?" asked Chelsea. "Maybe something in law. Perhaps I'll be the new Judge Judy," laughed her mom.

In the months before Maria's departure, Chelsea got closer to Jon. One day while shooting baskets outside, he admitted to Chelsea that despite appearing confident, he worried about the same things as she did. He had a tremendous fear of failure. Chelsea sympathized with him: "No one's perfect, Jon."

Jon also started spending more time in the kitchen. Maria smiled, "Bicho, let me show you how to fill and fold the pupusas." Chelsea was surprised at how quickly Jon got the knack of it. He particularly liked to stuff his own pupusas with huge amounts of chicken, black beans, and rice.

Maria's sudden departure from the Ryans' home seemed to put an end to these pleasant nights. A familiar chill enveloped the house, especially between her parents. Chelsea's past successful efforts to engage everyone failed, even when she cooked the family's favorite meals. She blamed the family's depression on Maria's departure. "They have finally realized how special Maria is," Chelsea thought. She forced herself to rationalize that Maria's life was improved, and that they would reconnect before her departure for college in the fall.

The summer months flew by for Chelsea. She worked as a counselor at a nearby college day camp. The emotional chill in her home grew so intense that Chelsea often spent weekends away, at the homes of her fellow counselors.

Before she knew it, late August arrived, and she was attending orientation at Southwynd College. The day before her departure for college, her family enjoyed a special dinner at a restaurant. The significance of this family system change seemed to revive the familial warmth that had waned. Her dad toasted over how proud he was as a parent at her decision to enter the medical field. At home, her mother insisted on picking out various wardrobes for Chelsea, and telling her how radiant she looked in them. Helene, however, could not prevent herself from telling her daughter to take her time before falling in love. Even Jon seemed excited about her college departure. He looked forward to visiting her some weekends and attending a few college basketball games.

On her first day at Southwynd, Chelsea was pleased to meet her roommate, Lucia, a fellow nursing student. Lucia was petite and attractive. A naturalized citizen, she lived in New York City but had originally come to the United States from Guatemala. Lucia later chuckled when she first heard Chelsea use Spanish terms like "bicha" and "dunndo." But she was very pleased to meet a classmate who loved tacos and empanadas as much as she did.

The roommates became fast friends. They helped each other traverse their courses in anatomy and microbiology during freshmen year. Chelsea often spoke of Maria, and eventually Lucia felt that she knew Maria personally from Chelsea's numerous stories. The girls formed a tight social circle with their fellow students, and the year quickly flew by in a blur of academics, winter carnivals, and frequent trips to the bars and restaurants in nearby Saratoga Springs. Chelsea was always careful to limit these soirees to two drinks for the night. Academically, Chelsea did well and made the Dean's List both semesters.

Surprisingly, that first year Chelsea found herself talking most often to her dad as he helped her with understanding medical diseases such as anemia and hypertension. He was pleased to patiently explain medical terms to her. Through him, she learned that her mom was enrolled at a local college in Boston. Both parents were very involved in Jon's stellar athletic junior year. He excelled in both basketball and baseball. Chelsea herself had attended a Christmas basketball tournament of Jon's, where he excelled on the court. He had a fiery and winning disposition on the court that earned the admiration of his teammates. Naturally, he was also dating the captain of the cheerleading squad.

For the summer break, Dr. Ryan had procured Chelsea a job as an aide at his hospital. Working at the bedside with nurses, Chelsea was filled with doubt. Nursing came with incredible responsibility. "What if I can't do a needle prick right and hurt the patient?" she worried. The nurses reassured her that they all initially had those fears. Chelsea could not help being impressed that everyone at the hospital, from custodians to nurses, had huge respect for her dad. The nurses all said that they preferred working with Dr. Ryan to all the other doctors. She was proud to be introduced as his daughter and enjoyed their frequent lunches together at the hospital.

Summer passed quickly, and Chelsea soon found herself back at college with Lucia. The girls had agreed that they would remain roommates. Lucia had also worked in a hospital that summer, in the Bronx. She lamented that others of her skin color, mostly very poor, often did not seek medical attention until a sickness was too far advanced. She hoped that one day she would be able to return to Guatemala in some capacity of preventive care.

Lucia's talk of Guatemala turned Chelsea's thoughts to Maria. Chelsea hoped that Maria and her family were healthy and happy. In fact, this past summer Chelsea had gone to Maria's old apartment, but to no avail. Maria, her children, and Ramon no longer lived there. The new occupants, another Hispanic family, told them they didn't know the Gomez family.

Sophomore year 2007 flew by as quickly as freshmen year had. Academics were more challenging, but Chelsea now possessed a confidence that went beyond academics. She had a better sense of herself and knew that she wanted a good career, and eventually a family in the future. But she was taking her mom's advice, and knew she had lots of time for that. That didn't stop her from meeting lots of boys, some of whom were very interested in getting to know her personally. Chelsea, however, preferred to socialize with a large group of nursing students.

From afar, Chelsea learned from her parents that Jon was drawing interest from colleges in his senior year. Coaches in both basketball and baseball showed interest especially because his academics were superior. While several large Ivy League teams recruited him, Jon and his dad wanted assurances that he could play right away in both sports. When these team representatives did not agree to his terms, Jon chose a prestigious "small" Ivy League Division III school, Winchester University in upstate Vermont. As his father had hoped, Jon majored in pre-med.

The summer prior to Chelsea's junior year was a happier one for the Ryan family. Her parents laughed about becoming "empty nesters," since both children would be away attending college. Dr. Ryan teased, "I can't think about retiring now with two college tuitions." Helene was taking classes at the local university, finishing her bachelor's degree. One night she announced to the family that she might like to enroll in law school. Her husband only laughed. "How are we going to travel if you are in law school?"

Chelsea again worked at the hospital that summer. Her colleagues were impressed by the growth of her nursing skills and hoped she would join them at the hospital one day. Her dad also seemed more relaxed, as the merger of the hospitals was complete. He could again concentrate on repairing the shoulders and knees of his patients.

Early junior year found Chelsea and Lucia conducting "practicals" at a hospital near the college. Chelsea drew blood for the first time and was happy to see her older gentleman patient barely wince.

It was almost Thanksgiving break, and Chelsea planned on returning home the Tuesday just before the holiday. She looked forward to seeing her brother, because with both school and sports, he had little time to talk to her. She knew that he had made the basketball team at college, and in fact had a game that Friday night. Chelsea thought before she went to bed that Friday night, with Jon's college being only two hours away, she could enjoy many future games in his career. Little did she know that soon her life would be irrevocably changed.

## Chapter 6: I Wish You Were Never Born

"GOOD LUCK TONIGHT," said Matt. Jon's roommate at Winchester College wished him well, for tonight was his first college basketball game. Jon had to admit that his first several weeks at college were emotionally freeing for him. He was away from his stifling family, and in particular his annoying mother. He now had begun his first tangible steps in his career objective to become a famous plastic surgeon.

As Jon walked to the athletic facility, he considered himself lucky to have Matt as a roommate. A fellow pre-med student, but not a student athlete, Matt offered to share his notes with Jon. So what if Matt was a bit "country" and frankly a bit goofy. He would be most helpful.

So happy was Jon that he had not thought about his mother's haunting words for a week or so; the words that had defined him since they were uttered: "I wish you were never born." If Jon were honest with himself, he would say he hated his mother; this woman who would deny him birth when others recognized his unique athletic and academic abilities. No, hate was too strong a word – she annoyed him. But he laughed to himself as he thought that hate was probably the right word for her immigrant family, especially his grandfather. He clearly remembered his mother's crude father, in poor English, ordering his meek wife to pour him more wine. The old man in his stained clothes with holes in his shirt. Jon could never forget his grandfather's rough bricklayer hands grabbing his cheek. No one else understood why he never wanted to visit his grandparents' Connecticut home.

Jon greeted his new teammates at the walk-through practice. His coach, Jim Johnson, who had ardently recruited Jon, emphasized conquering first-game jitters. Coach Johnson pulled Jon aside and said he might get playing time tonight. While Jon smiled at him, inwardly he said to himself, "Soon I'll be starting."

Jon was pleased with his new teammates, many of whom were upper classmen. They seemed to appreciate his talents. Jon hoped that they turned out better than his high school teammates. Captain of both his baseball and basketball teams his high school junior year, he was not elected captain of either team his

senior year. Imagine, Jon reflected, the only player to get a scholarship, and his teammates did not recognize him.

Jon agreed with his dad that it was all jealously on the part of his teammates. They rejected his abilities and, truth be told, probably his good looks too. They were envious that he always dated the best-looking girls. If he saw his high school teammates on the street, Jon vowed he would walk right by them.

Following practice, Jon walked back to the dorm with his new teammates. They agreed to have plenty of beer available tonight after their victory. They teased him about his pretty new girlfriend. One said, "Don't let her get away. We might swarm in. "With three hours to kill before the bus left for nearby Carlton College, Jon called Cindy, and they agreed to meet for lunch at the Commons in about an hour. Cindy was a Californian blonde whom he had met at freshman orientation. Even though they had known each other only seven weeks, it was an intense relationship. They had already been intimate. There was one problem: Jon found her to be "clingy," constantly on him to be "exclusive." That was not going to happen, Jon told himself. He liked Cindy, but he liked more the admiration of his roommates for dating the long-legged blonde.

Alone in his room, as often happened, something again triggered his relationship with his mother. She simply did not understand him. What was the big deal in hiding Maria's handbag before she was to go home? It was just a joke. But not to his mother, who'd pulled a nutter. He smiled as he thought of the deed. Even goody-two-shoes Chelsea yelled at him after that one. Similarly, "Helene" went nuts after learning he gave Maria's son Roberto a wedgie one day. She didn't see the humor in Roberto's underwear being pulled up to his neck. It was crazy.

Jon knew his dad understood him. It was as if the two of them were one. Dad's only problem was Mom. His dad simply gave in to her too much – like the time Jon was forced to go see that stupid shrink. As for his sister, Chelsea, she was okay, but far too soft for his liking. Sometimes Jon felt that she cared more about Maria, than about him. She was always going on about how wonderful Maria's

pupusas were. She didn't seem to realize that Maria was okay, but she was just a housekeeper.

Jon closed his eyes and tried to put his home life out of his mind. He was free from that now. Someday he would be an in-demand plastic surgeon who would restore the beauty in others. People would fawn over his considerable skills and be envious of him. He would not be stupid like his father and lend his skills to a teaching hospital. No, he would be paid very well for his skills.

Try as he might, however, Jon could not push out the thought that his mother never really wanted him. He recalled the day she uttered those infamous words.

It happened while Jon was in middle school. Picking Jon up from school one day, his mother spotted a kitten. It was not a pretty house kitten, but a scrawny, smelly runaway. His mother insisted on taking it home, with Jon squirming away from the creature as they drove. When they arrived home, Jon's father placated his mother and agreed to the kitten's "adoption." Jon was upset at his father's approval of the kitten, and to Jon's dismay, the kitten soon became a member of the family.

One day when his mom was out, Jon picked up the kitten by the scruff of the neck and gazed at it. He had never even touched the animal before. He filled a bucket with water and dunked the creature. He did this several times, for longer and longer intervals, until his mother unexpectedly returned home. Witnessing his actions, Helene screamed, "What's wrong with you, Jon!" followed by "I wish I never had you." Repulsed, she quickly gathered up the kitten, turned her back on Jon, and walked away.

Returning to the present, Jon felt fresh perspiration on his forehead as he lay in his dorm room. What his mother, and frankly no one, understood was that he had not been trying to kill the kitten. He had merely wanted to observe the reaction of the creature. His stupid mother did not understand this. But Jon remembered that his father had come to his defense. Dr. Ryan joked that Jon was simply giving the kitten a bath.

This did not placate his mother, who was concerned and took Jon to a therapist. He remembered having to sit with this ugly dude with glasses and talk about his life. The counselor thought he could fool Jon into saying something stupid. Jon considered it a "cat and mouse" game where he outsmarted the shrink. Fortunately, after several of these inane sessions, Jon's dad agreed that he did not have to continue. After that, Jon and his mother did not speak to each other for three months. Jon did not consider their argument his fault. For that matter, Jon recalled that his mother did not speak to her husband for the same length of time.

Noticing the time, Jon jumped out of bed and packed up his uniform. He was soon on his way to the Commons, where he was greeted with a deep kiss from Cindy. During lunch, Cindy resumed her campaign that they become exclusive, which irritated Jon. "Why can't you commit to me, Jon?" Cindy sighed. Jon wanted to tell her how stupid she sounded, but he simply smirked.

As Cindy spoke, Jon's attention turned to her mouth—more specifically, to her mouth full of gum. This was not regular gum, mind you, but bubble gum; bubble gum that she constantly popped as she spoke. In fact, Jon was disgusted as she continued to chew gum, even as she ate her cheeseburger. It bothered Jon so much that he wanted to slap the gum out of her mouth. "Not again," he thought.

Jon had regretted an incident that happened a week ago. Cindy and Jon had been walking on campus after a late night of studying at the library. That was when the argument started. Cindy threatened that if they were not "exclusive," she might date someone else. Cindy seemed to brag to Jon that Kurt, Jon's basketball teammate and captain of the team, had asked her out. In a flash, Jon struck out at

Cindy, and stopped her from talking further. He didn't even remember the slap, only Cindy's reaction. She looked startled and afraid. He'd profusely apologized to Cindy. After some effort on his part, she gave in and returned his hugs.

Today, after her plea, Jon decided to appease her by agreeing that they would be "officially dating." Giving Cindy a quick kiss, Jon promised to see her later at the "victory" party after the game. Little did Jon know that he would never make that party.

# Chapter 7: Murder on Campus

ORAZIO "ROCKY" CONLEY groggily answered the 4 a.m. phone call. "This is not good," he thought as his wife also awakened. He heard the gruff voice of his boss, Colonel David Saunders of the Vermont State Police, informing him that there had been a murder at Winchester College. Murders were rare in Vermont's Cheshire County, where "crimes" often involved impaired skiers or arguments between bad neighbors. Even more troubling was that the murder involved a college basketball player close to his own son's age. Colonel Saunders told Rocky that their investigative team was already on site, as this was beyond the scope of the small Winchester Police Department.

"Okay, I'll be there in about an hour."

His wife, Nancy, immediately recognized the significance of this death. "That could have been one of our kids," she sighed.

"I know," said Rocky, giving her a quick kiss. In a matter of minutes, he was on his way to the scene.

Rocky Conley was the lead criminal investigative attorney for the Vermont State Police Unit. At the age of 55, he was nearing mandatory retirement. Rocky was a large-boned man and had the thick build of the former athlete that he was. People often teased him about his unique name, but where he grew up, Italian mothers and Irish fathers were common. He reflected this ethnicity with a large Roman nose that, broken so often playing sports, was his predominant feature. His Irish side was revealed by his burnt red hair, now sprinkled with gray. Although he was not conventionally handsome, his features merged together into a pleasant face that made it easy for people to talk to him.

Rocky's easygoing demeanor combined with his physical presence had helped him solve many crimes. His colleagues often teased him, remarking that he could even get a priest to reveal someone's confession. While some criminal investigators concentrated on the five "W's" or the textbook motive, opportunity, and means, Rocky worked from the victim out. His approach was to learn everything he could about the victim, and then work out toward the people in the victim's sphere. Rocky would then use his street knowledge of people to absorb everything about them. He noticed everything beyond words – a blush of the skin, the averted gaze, even the hair rising on the accused's arm – to complete his portrait of the suspect. He once got a local farmer to confess to murdering a neighbor using his unique insight. The farmer was convinced that Rocky understood how someone who'd trespassed on his property deserved to die.

Rocky always felt that growing up in Everett, Massachusetts, an industrial city just north of Boston, provided him with a street-level doctorate education. He grew up with similar working-class children whose Irish, Italian, and African American fathers fought in WWII. These fathers were often his coaches, and their wives were wonderful cooks who often served melt-in-your-mouth meatballs in their simple kitchens. Rocky's dad worked in nearby Charlestown's Navy Yard, just steps away from where the colonists fought the British in 1776. That feisty spirit continued in Everett, where Rocky and his friends played with and fought other kids in the city's playgrounds.

As Rocky drove to the scene, he recognized the irony that both he and the victims were from Massachusetts. However, their respective towns could not be more different. Wellesley's affluence often hid people's demons behind fancy clothes and mansions. Everett's gritty population often went the opposite route and bore a cynicism that almost expected the worst in people. But they could detect a phony as clearly as the superstitious could spot a black cat. Rocky's absorption of all the personalities he grew up with, both good and bad, gave him a sixth sense about someone's character. He always thanked Everett for this free education.

Rocky knew that if he wanted to go to college, sports would be his only ticket. The oldest of five siblings, Rocky started selling newspapers at age nine. He also started playing football at that young age. They say that in Everett, every son gets a football in his crib rather than a teddy bear. Everett had won more state football championships than nearly any other city or town in Massachusetts. In fact, in 1914, when Woodrow Wilson was President, the Everett team was considered the greatest high school football team of all times. They outscored their opponents 600 to 0 in a 13-game schedule played throughout the country.

In this football culture, Rocky started making a name for himself early. In fact his nickname, given at age nine, was originated by a coach who professed he hit like a rock; hence the name "Rocky," which stuck. Rocky became a star runningback, known to run through rather than around opponents. He ran so well that he got the attention of college recruiters his senior year. One of those recruiters was from the team Rocky had revered since his youth – the Syracuse Orange, home of the great runningback Jim Brown. Thus, Rocky was thrilled to accept a scholarship from Syracuse University.

Although his college football career did not work out as he had hoped, with a change of coach his sophomore year and soon after a knee injury derailing his career, he still managed to play sporadically for four years. On the positive side, he met his wife Julie, a Vermont native, at Syracuse. After college, they moved back to Vermont, where Rocky attended law school. Shortly after he became a lawyer, he and Julie got married. Julie procured a teaching job at a local elementary school, and Rocky started work as an assistant district attorney, prosecuting cases. Eventually, he got the attention of Colonel Saunders, who asked him to join his office. He was now the lead investigator for the homicide unit. After raising two children who were now attending college, Rocky and his wife were looking forward to retirement in five years or so.

When Rocky got to the crime scene, his lead assistant, Dean Edwards, had already secured the area. He was interviewing some of Jon's distraught teammates while other personnel photographed the area. Jon's body had not yet been removed by the Medical Examiner. Rocky lifted the sheet and gazed at the handsome visage of the slain youth. Rocky almost broke down, as he thought this could easily have been his own son. Sympathy welled within him for this young man's parents, who he learned were already on their way to Vermont. Rocky observed that Jon appeared to have two bullet wounds from a small-caliber gun. One had hit him in the leg, and the other had entered the back of his head.

The investigator immediately thought that this was an assassination and probably had been planned for some time. He at once told Dean to put as many police as could be spared on toll booths leading away from the college, and to especially be on the lookout for vehicles with single occupants. Dean said, "Already been done." Rocky also prepared himself for the media onslaught that awaited them the next day. These types of targeted murders on college campuses just don't happen in rural Vermont.

Rocky called his team together at 9 a.m. at State Police Headquarters. He had to fight his way through the media and cameras, telling everyone he would have a statement later that day. Besides Inspector Dean Edwards, Rocky was joined by his forensic expert, Kim Fiorentino. She had already confiscated Jon's cell phone and computer for analysis. Another inspector, Sonny Parker, would be doing grunt work securing videotapes from the college security system, which hopefully would be a huge advantage in the investigation. He and Dean would also conduct the ballistics investigation that day. Inspector Parker would interview anyone on the campus who may have had information both before and after the murder. Lastly was assistant district attorney Meredith Marshall, who would prepare any search warrants and charges against the suspect. Rocky learned that the medical examiner would have a preliminary report that afternoon.

The mood in the room was somber as Rocky addressed his upset team. "So what do we know so far?" Dean explained that it was a bit of a head-scratcher. Jon was a freshman who had been on campus all of three months. He was popular and seemingly well-liked, and his teammates said he had no altercations on or off the court.

Dean informed the squad that Jon's basketball team had just played their first game at nearby Carlton College. Jon had actually played a bit in the game – unusual for a freshman – and played well, according to his coach. The team had arrived back on campus about 10:30 p.m., and Jon's teammates were anxious to get back to the dormitory and shower. Jon had to go back to his locker and told his teammates he would see them in Malloy (the dorm) shortly. He never made it. Jon was shot only steps away from the locker rooms, which were close to the college library on the vast campus.

Rocky interspersed his report with directives. "Make sure we interview everyone at the library – staff and students alike. The shooter may have staked out the situation there. Also interview campus security for any reports of unusual people on campus in recent weeks."

Rocky questioned his team, "Have we found out if anyone heard gunshots?"

"Yes, a couple of students recall hearing two shots. Unfortunately, they thought it was nearby hunters and did not call campus security. Jon was not found until 1:30 a.m. when campus security was making a routine check of the grounds."

Rocky said aloud what the team immediately knew -the shooter had a three-hour head start on law enforcement. "Okay, let's get to work and meet again in the a.m." Rocky held out a picture of Jon. "Let's give these parents some relief, and solve this case quickly," he said as the determined team nodded. "I'm meeting his parents later today."

"Meredith, may I have a word with you?"

Rocky and the district attorney's office had worked collaboratively in the past, but attorney Meredith Marshall was his favorite. "Any suggestions about questioning his parents today?"

She responded, "Obviously, take your cues from how they are handling this crisis, but they are our best resource. You know you will have the full cooperation of this office to put this perpetrator away forever."

"Thank you, Meredith."

Rocky promptly got up to speed on the Ryan family, who it seemed were both well-liked and well respected. He had already received calls from the Massachusetts State Police offering assistance. Television cameras had already encamped at the family's Wellesley home. Jon's handsome face was in news reports in both states, given the unusual nature of the murder. Rocky learned that Jon was a popular pre-med student who seemed well-liked by everyone.

Rocky had a 5 p.m. meeting with Dr. and Mrs. Ryan, who were being driven to Vermont by State Police. He was surprised then to find Jon's sister, Chelsea Ryan, in his office at 4 p.m. Through tears she explained that she attended college in nearby New York and had decided to come directly. Dispatching with protocol, he immediately hugged this sobbing, sweet girl who could easily pass for his daughter.

Rocky got Chelsea a coffee, and when she was able, simply asked her to tell him about her brother. "He was going to help people as a physician, like my dad," blurted Chelsea. He identified with Chelsea when she said, "Everything came easy for Jon, not like me." He liked this young woman already.

Soon Chelsea was joined by her distraught parents. They crumpled in each other's arms while Rocky briefly left the room. Somewhat composed and holding his wife's hand, Dr. Ryan asked what the police had learned. Rocky informed them that these first forty-eight hours were crucial. "Since last night, we have had police staking out major roadways away from town. My team has been interviewing everyone on and around the campus, and we are collecting forensic information."

By this time, Rocky had also gotten some ballistic information that he shared with the family. His team had collected two bullets that appeared to come from a .38 caliber revolver. Mrs. Ryan wept and asked if her son's face was damaged. Rocky understood her question and said he did not know but would find out.

Rocky kept to himself that he had been surprised by the gun used in the crime. Sometimes called a Saturday night special, these inexpensive guns were often involved in crimes in the inner city, where guns were easily bought and sold. A professional assassin would never use this type of gun because of its spotty performance.

Rocky now asked the family if they knew anyone who would want to hurt Jon. Dr. Ryan almost shouted, "This is what I don't understand! Everyone loved Jon. He had no serious breakups with girlfriends or friends." As Dr. Ryan talked, Rocky observed that Mrs. Ryan looked away, almost as if she was in deep thought. He made a mental note to follow up with her. Outwardly, however, she and Chelsea agreed that Jon had no enemies. Dr. Ryan just kept repeating, "He was a star."

As the Ryans left the office to go to the Medical Examiner's office and make funeral plans, Rocky told them he would remain in close contact. He also relayed to Helene that most of the damage was to the rear of Jon's head.

Later that night, Rocky received some preliminary information from Investigators Dean and Sonny. For hours they had reviewed all of the cameras from the night of the murder. Unfortunately, the area near the locker rooms was poorly lit and had only one camera to review. Rocky watched as a shadowy figure fired one shot, paused, and then fired another at a figure emerging from the locker room. Even Jon could not be identified from this poor-quality tape. The shooter then disappeared from view, and was not seen again. They all lamented that Winchester College's security cameras were not all working.

Dean and Sonny noted that what was unusual from the tapes was that no one was seen leaving the campus at the time of the murder. Thus begged the question: how and where did the suspect leave town? As Rocky pondered this question, he considered that maybe the suspect did not leave town.

Day two of the investigation found Rocky receiving pressure from all fronts. Colonel

Saunders, normally unfazed, said that the governor wanted a progress update. Both Rocky and the colonel conducted an interview with the media. The obviously frustrated media wanted details that Rocky could not reveal about an investigation in progress. Dr. Ryan was also demanding more information, and Rocky promised to keep Jon's father informed of any developments.

Rocky learned that Jon's body had been released to the family, who planned a funeral on Wednesday of that week. The Ryan family knew that hundreds of colleagues, friends, and teammates would attend a public funeral that they were not capable of enduring. Therefore, they planned a private viewing and a Catholic Mass for Jon, with a local burial.

The investigators got their first break when on the following Monday, a library worker reported that she had seen an unfamiliar man in the library. Normally only students were allowed, and they needed a passkey to enter. She remembered this gentleman because he asked if he could enter because his daughter was thinking of attending the college. The worker allowed him admittance and recalled that the man, perhaps somewhere in his late forties, was of medium height and build. He was dark-skinned and had an accent, maybe

Mexican or South American. The library worker agreed to work with a composite artist.

By the end of the day, the police as well as the media were given this composite picture. News stations across the Northeast shared the photo, as the public was intrigued by this case of the murdered athlete.

On that Tuesday, Rocky and his team got another break. A local convenience store employee ten miles away in the village of Fairfax remembered seeing a man who matched this description. The man had walked in looking somewhat unkempt, and had purchased water and food. The clerk recalled that the man did not appear to have a vehicle, since he walked down the road when he left the store.

Rocky immediately sent a S.W.A.T. team to the area, intentionally avoiding any media attention. Out of respect for Jon's funeral, he did not want a media circus, especially if the tip did not work out. Within hours, and with the assistance of dogs, the team had spotted a tent in an isolated area of rugged terrain. The police surrounded the tent with guns drawn and told whoever was there to come out. A middle-aged man matching the description came out with his hands up.

# Chapter 8: The Murder Interrogation

THE DAY AFTER JON'S MURDER, Rocky Conley found himself face to face with Ramon Gomez. Ramon kept looking at his hands as if believing they were not capable of his act. Rocky absorbed those gnarled hands and thought, "This is a man used to hard labor."

Ramon suddenly shouted, "This should have never happened. We are a good family." As he spoke, he pounded the table with those strong hands. Always wanting to stay in control of the encounter, Rocky instinctively lightly touched Ramon's hands. "It's okay, Ramon," he said in a soft voice. "Here, take a sip of this. It's Spanish coffee." As Ramon took a small sip, a smile emerged. He could taste the difference between this and "Americano" coffee.

Rocky then began the interview, as he did with any suspect. His methods were: Give them a broad general question and build some sort of rhythm to their dynamic. Allow the suspect to initially do most of the talking, and most importantly, observe everything. How does the suspect refer to himself? What is he saying nonverbally, i.e. is he sweating, nervous, making gestures? What do his eyes say?

Rocky had to let Ramon know that he was with someone capable of understanding him. He began, "I know you were born in El Salvador. Tell me about your life there." Ramon's mind easily went back to the place he never wanted to leave – his family farm. Soon he was sharing the names of his family members. Rocky urged him on, "Oh I see – you wanted to be a farmer like your dad." "Yes," conceded Ramon. "That's all I ever wanted - to grow corn and tobacco with my family."

No longer rubbing his hands together, Ramon actually leaned back to answer Rocky's next question. Ramon seemed to be appraising Rocky as much as Rocky was assessing him. "Tell me how you got to America."

"My family had a good life. We had everything we ever wanted. But we were not left in peace. The army killed whoever they wanted. Soon our neighbors were fighting with us if we did not pick up a gun."

"I heard that America was the place to be free. There, soldiers or communists could not control your life. I was the strongest, so I went first to America. I started sending money to bring my sister Maria, my brother Luis, and my parents here." Rocky was impressed that Ramon had emerged with a plan to save the family. "But," said Ramon, almost to himself, "I failed everyone."

Making a mental note to return to this "failure" theme, Rocky continued his general questioning. "Tell me how you got here. I don't know if I would have had the courage to leave a place I loved, Ramon."

Ramon responded to the apparent concern of this detective. "I hired a coyote to take me from my country to the border. It cost me $3,000. In our group, there were ten people — two El Salvadorans about my age, and two families. One family had two sons, probably about six and eight years of age. The other family had a baby about two years old. The coyote was happy to collect his ransom, but he asked if the baby was strong enough for the long trip. The baby's father said they had no choice, because the family would be killed if they stayed in El Salvador."

Ramon told Rocky that after several days together, he grew closer to the two families. He learned that the parents of the two-year-old had been threatened by the group opposed to the government. The father who declared his two-year-old was strong enough told Ramon, "My father is a police officer. The neighbors blamed me when someone disappeared. We were told by 'la communist' that we would be killed if we didn't leave." The other parents with the older children told Ramon they were also threatened. "I was on my farm," the father said, "when the Federales visited. They handed me a gun and told me to fight or my sons would disappear."

Inoculated from this type of cultural violence, Rocky asked Ramon if the families also made it across to America. Ramon smiled as his thoughts brought him some pride, even if he now was a murderer. Then he continued his story.

"On the tenth day, somewhere in Mexico, our coyote disappeared. We woke up with nothing but our clothes and three canteens of water. One of the mothers cried, 'What happens to us now!' None of us knew how to answer her. We decided to follow the sun and head north. The older men constantly pushed the families to move quickly. 'Pronto, pronto.' At one point, I ordered the men to stop. The three young children were exhausted."

"The next morning, the sun was not yet up when I heard stirring. The families were fast asleep, but the two men urged me to go with them. 'You will never make it with the ninos.' I knew they were probably right. We could all die wandering in the desert. But I could not leave them. No! I told them. The men laughed at me and called me loco."

"As they raced off, I noticed they had taken all the water. I ran after them and was able to tackle the slower thief, who had one canteen of water. I yelled, 'God will curse you!' and kicked him. Then he got up, and both of these heartless men ran off into the desert."

"As the families woke to all the noise, I spoke to the fathers. 'I will not leave you,' I told them. I gave the only canteen to one of the dads, and told him to just give enough to your ninos so they don't suffer."

"The families followed me north. Our travel was slow, as the late morning heat was unbearable. We would gather under a large cactus for any shade we could find. My heart melted when I heard one of the boys ask his mother, 'Will we ever get to America?'"

As Ramon continued his story, Rocky learned that after two more days of oppressive heat followed by cold nights, the families were unable to rise on the third day. Their bodies shaded by a giant cactus, the two fathers said their families could go no further. Ramon watched them drinking from the canteen. Knowing their water was getting very low, he refused to take a sip. He realized he must get the families help. Making mental notes of the mountain ridge and other landmarks, Ramon told the families to remain where they were. He told them he would get help, but he was not sure they even believed him.

Ramon wandered for three full days in the sweltering desert. He fantasized about the cold, refreshing homemade ice creams his mother gave him as a child. His swollen tongue released no moisture, even with visions of the mouthwatering food. He slept for only a few hours a night, foolishly believing he could navigate his way north by the stars. By the fourth day, his eyes were almost blinded shut. His fingers did not bend and his legs were numb.

The next thing Ramon remembered, he was lying prone over a mustang's back. His pony was led by a large white horse, occupied by a man with a massive girth. The man wore a white cowboy hat and a white matching shirt. Ramon drifted in and out of consciousness. He remembered the man putting water to his lips and gently urging him to sip.

Ramon's next memory was lying on crisp sheets that smelled like lavender. He was clean and wearing pajamas twice his size. He looked up to see the face of the large man with a white handlebar mustache. "We must get to the people in the desert," implored Ramon. Concerned, the man asked, "How many?" "Four adults and three young children." "Are you okay to travel?" said the man. Ramon rose to his feet, only to fall to the floor in a heap. He stood up and forced himself to dress, holding on to the bed.

The white-haired savior, who said, "Call me Don," met Ramon outside near the paddock. Don had procured five ponies and some provisions for the trip. Don said, "I can take you where I found you." Ramon hoped he remembered some of the landmarks.

Soon they were at the spot where Ramon was found. Ramon recited a prayer to the Madonna, and looked over the barren land of the desert. Everything looked the same – all blue and brown hues. He had spent most of his life in the mountains, surrounded by fertile, lush green land. Right then, he may as well have been on the moon. For some reason

Ramon felt a pull to the east, and he pointed in that direction.

At one point in the journey, two of the ponies, sensing something, jumped up on their hind legs. Don scoured the landscape with his eyes, and then pointing due east, he exclaimed, "What is that orange thing?" Ramon remembered that the older boy had an orange Arizona State Aztec tee shirt. Don and Ramon raced to the location. They found all seven people alive, but the two-year-old was unconscious.

Ramon watched the remarkable work of Don. He helped Ramon take all of the people to his home. He restored the baby's temperature with a tub of ice. As he made all of them comfortable and brought them food, he cautioned everyone to eat and drink slowly, so as not to overwhelm their bodies. "You will be fine here with me," Don assured them all.

For two days, Ramon watched this kind man care for eight strangers. Ramon thought to himself, "This is a man of few words. He does not smile often, as if he is used to sadness." One morning Don took Ramon out for a horse ride. Don proudly pointed and said, "That is all mine." Ramon looked to the vista as Don waved his hand. It was then Ramon realized that Don's land extended as far as the eye could see. "Do you have family?" Ramon asked. "Not now," responded the rancher, and he turned his horse to head back.

On the third day, Don called the families together. "The Border Patrol wants me to turn you back. I don't think that's right. You have come so far. My land ends at the United States border. I will take you to a break in the fence and help you to sneak through." Upon hearing this, one of the mothers tried to kiss the hands of "E'l Angel." He said nothing, but his red face reflected his embarrassment.

As promised, Don took them to the border, providing them with two days' worth of food and water. As each member of the group navigated through the fence, the rancher told them, "Work hard and obey the laws, and you will succeed in America."

After hearing Ramon's story, Rocky, for one of the few times in his career, found himself losing control of an interview. He wanted to know more about these remarkable people that Ramon had traveled with. He knew the focus of the interview was whether Ramon had committed murder. But he felt a strong regard for this man, and what he'd went through to come to this country.

"Tell me about Jon Ryan, Ramon." Ramon again looked away but caressed his hands again and again. Rocky thought, "Perhaps he is trying to cleanse them." Ramon finally spoke. "This should not have happened, none of it. We came to this country and worked hard. We never broke the law. We were good Americans, as good as the rancher who helped us told us to be."

Ramon's face tightened. "He should not have touched my niece like that." Then Ramon described the abuse that left his niece Alisa in tears in the Ryan home. "I should never have listened to my sister. I wanted us to go to the police, but my sister loved the Ryan family so much that she trusted them to do the right thing. Next thing we knew, the Federal agents ordered us shipped back to El Salvador. I would not go. I had to save them here."

Over the next two hours, a confused Rocky pieced together the chain of events that had resulted in Jon's murder. Rocky was instinctively suspicious of the immigration agents who got the family to move within twenty-four hours. "The only reason my sister Maria agreed to the plan was because those agents said they would help her get back to America legally," said Ramon.

Ramon tearfully told Rocky how helpless he felt about his sister's family when they were returned to El Salvador. "My brother-in-law

Carlos was killed, like my brother Luis. The gangs threatened my family every day." Alone in the States and helpless, Ramon's anger built to a point that he could not control. "I began to plot my 'la venganza'," he said.

Rocky, having already given his Miranda warning, again counseled Ramon that he did not have to say more. "No," said Ramon, "I will give the confession. That boy deserved to die." Ramon then signed a written confession detailing his purchase of the gun, the stalking of Jon, and how he pumped two shots into Jon on the college campus.

Following the interview, Rocky shook Ramon's hand. He did not do that with many murderers. Rocky then sought out his boss, Colonel Saunders of the Vermont State Police. The colonel commended Rocky on his fine work. It seemed to Rocky that his boss would be relieved to have the media and political pressure eased with Ramon's confession.

"There's something strange about this case, Colonel," said Rocky. "Ramon's family might have had some fraud perpetrated against them to get them deported. I want to investigate Dr. Ryan and his family. There may be mitigating factors here." Colonel Saunders seemed anxious to leave. "I heard something about the circumstances. We can talk about it tomorrow."

The next morning, Rocky arrived in his office early. He wanted to go to Wellesley as soon as possible. He couldn't get the image of immigration officials hustling a family away in the midst of sexual abuse charges out of his mind. Something did not make sense. Rocky felt his familiar sports adrenaline kick in as he was determined to find out the truth.

At 9 a.m., Rocky was called into Colonel Saunders' office. Sitting there were three stern-faced men. The long faces on Colonel Saunders, the state police commissioner, and the attorney general told Rocky that something was wrong. Colonel Sanders spoke first: "The case is over, Rocky. Ramon's court-appointed attorney will agree to a second-degree murder plea agreement. He will get twenty years, and with good behavior might be out in fifteen years."

Rocky forced himself to sit down. This "deal" went against everything he stood for in his work. He challenged the men, "What if the story about the deportation is true?" The men's stern faces were unmoved. Rocky had been in enough of these bureaucratic meetings to know not to argue. The die had been cast.

All he did know was that some powerful people had pulled strings here.

Rocky was about to leave when he turned to Colonel Saunders. He had to ask, "Does the Ryan family even know that Ramon killed their son?" "No," responded Rocky's boss. "I need you to tell them about the arrest. They also have to be informed of this plea agreement and approve it. We think, given the circumstances, they will agree. Can you speak to them tomorrow, Rocky?"

Rocky left the meeting and immediately opened the neck of his button-down shirt. Whether metaphysically or not, the collar had almost squeezed his Adam's apple. "I don't like it when the rules don't apply to everyone," he muttered.

"Ramon had more fiber in his body than the people in that room."

The next day, Rocky prepared for the difficult drive to the Ryan home. On his way out the door, he spotted assistant district attorney Meredith Marshall just getting out of her car. She shared an affinity with Rocky, as she had also had Jon's case taken away from her. "Some case, Meredith," Rocky commented. She responded, "It's nice to have friends in high places." Rocky probed, "Who are these friends?" "I don't know all of them, Rocky, but

I heard one name prominently – Ed Corcoran. He's a private investigator in Boston." "Thanks, Meredith," said Rocky. As he walked away, Rocky said to himself, "I need to find out more about this Ed Corcoran guy."

# Chapter 9: The Denial

EARLY THE DAY AFTER JON'S FUNERAL, Detective Rocky Conley called the Ryan home. He told the family that the police had arrested someone for Jon's murder, and asked if he could drive down and talk to the family

Several hours later, Rocky found himself in the kitchen of Dr. Ryan's expansive colonial home in a tony section of the town. The family was all present and immediately wanted to know the suspect's name. "Ramon Gomez," said Rocky as he sipped a cup of coffee. Initially the name did not register with Chelsea, but then it quickly hit her: Maria's brother! She gasped Maria's name. Puzzled about why Chelsea had screamed, Chelsea's parents had no initial reaction. Their minds were so filled with grief that they didn't process the familiar name. Finally, Chelsea watched as her ratcheted mother wailed to her father, "This is all your fault!" Chelsea jumped up, "What do you mean?" Then, turning to her father, she screamed, "What happened?" All color had drained from her father's stunned face as he slowly removed his glasses and rubbed his head. Rocky uncomfortably watched this family drama in silence. At last, Dr. Ryan turned to Rocky. "Have you interviewed this Ramon?"

"Yes, we interviewed him all night. He has confessed to the crime."

Seeming to process this information, Dr. Ryan asked Rocky if he could have some time alone with his family. Rocky agreed and said he would come back in a couple of hours.

When Rocky had left, Helene angrily demanded that her husband tell Chelsea the whole terrible story. Chelsea's head swiveled from one parent to the other as she yelled, "What is it?" It was her mother who spoke first. "One day a tearful Maria came to us and told us that her daughter Alisa had been 'touched' by Jon. We didn't know exactly what had happened, but I wanted to call the police." As spittle and tears streaked her face, Helene told Chelsea that her father's choice was to have Maria and her family removed. Dr. Ryan, whose face seemed to age ten years as he sat in the kitchen, uttered over and over, "He didn't touch that girl."

Chelsea felt her body and mind shutting down as she collapsed in her mother's lap. "So that's why Maria left so quickly," Chelsea murmured. Trying to process this, Chelsea thought, "Why would Alisa say this? Why didn't my parents try to find out if it was true?"

Finally, she shouted at her dad, "Why did you have them deported?"

"I didn't have them deported," said Dr. Ryan, defending himself. I simply told an immigration officer that they were illegal. They were spreading lies that Jon did something terrible."

The Ryan family sat in silence for several minutes, Chelsea caressed in her mother's arms. This family system was coming to terms with the ugly truth that it had been responsible somehow for Jon's death. At length, Chelsea examined the face of her dad, a face that she and so many others had once admired. At this moment she felt only hatred for that face as she stated, "Jon should be alive today!" Dr. Ryan got up and left the house in silence.

Rocky later told Chelsea and Helene that Ramon had given a full confession to authorities the previous night. He had no real plan to escape following the murder. In his parlance, "la venganza," or revenge, had to occur because of what had befallen his family in El Salvador. Chelsea learned that Carlos had passed away in the city of San Salvador where they lived. Rocky said that he did not know much more about Maria's children, except that they lived with her in that city.

Before Rocky left the Ryans, he explained the plea agreement that had been reached with Ramon, subject to their approval. Helene whispered, "I don't care. It won't bring my son back." Dr. Ryan later called Rocky and said the family did not object to the settlement.

The day after the traumatic meeting with the Ryan family, Rocky could not get the name of Ed Corcoran out of his mind. Just what had this guy done to engineer so much pain in the litany of candidates – from Ramon to the Ryans? And how much power did this guy have to simply make the legal case go away?

As he drove back to Vermont, these thoughts and more went through Rocky's head. In New Hampshire, he turned his car around. He had to go see this Ed Corcoran. To hell with his bosses and their deals.

Soon Rocky found himself in the plush Boston offices of Edward Corcoran and Associates. He was met by the pleasant face of the receptionist at the entrance. "Do you have an appointment?" she asked.

"I'm a district attorney on a case from Vermont that involves Mr. Corcoran." "Please take a seat, and I'll find out if he's in," she directed him.

An hour later, the irritated Rocky asked the not-so-pleasant receptionist for the fifth time if Mr. Corcoran knew he was waiting. "I'm sorry," she said tersely, "Mr. Corcoran is in meetings all day. He suggested you call and make an appointment."

The agitated Rocky could feel his athletic juices flowing as he drove the five hours back to Vermont. The juices were flowing so well for Rocky that he had to make five pit stops on the trip. And Ed Corcoran was not far from Rocky's thoughts throughout the drive. He would make it a personal mission to find out exactly what this "fixer" had done. In Rocky's mind, someone had to pay beyond Ramon and Jon for this tragic set of circumstances.

A week later Rocky, stood waiting outside the offices of Edward Corcoran and Associates. A lanky, gray-haired man with a quick stride was soon passing by him. By now Rocky knew who and what this man was all about.

"Are you Ed Corcoran?" Rocky called to the man. "Who's asking?" responded the man, barely slowing his stride. "Rocky Conley, the DA from Vermont. I tried to see you at your office the other day." Rocky's appearance did force Ed Corcoran to stop and take notice of him. He noticed the DA's intense eyes. "Sorry about that," Ed apologized, "You can imagine how busy this place can get. Did you make an appointment for today?"

"No, but I just need half an hour of your time," said Rocky. "Well, is this an official visit? Do you have a subpoena?" "No," said Rocky, "I just want to talk to you about the Ryan case." Ed Corcoran started walking hurriedly away. "Well, make an appointment and we can talk."

Just as Ed was about to enter the office building, Rocky called out, "Okay, and next time I'll bring Jim Popeo and Phil Strong. " Ed froze hearing those names, the door halfway open. For ten seconds he did not move. Rocky could almost hear the tumblers turning in his head. Then Ed turned to Rocky and said, "Come in."

It was a different Edward Corcoran who ushered Rocky into his grand office. Through the large windows, Rocky could see the foaming, gruff seas of Boston Harbor, as even the busy seagulls sensed a change in the air. Ed offered Rocky a seat and called to his secretary, "Janice, please get Mr. Conley – can I call you Rocky? – a cup of coffee."

Rocky disliked this man even more now and got right to the point. "I know you hired Jim Popeo and Phil Strong to act as immigration officials to trick the Gomez family into going back to El Salvador. I just want to know why you did it. Why not find out if the Ryan boy molested the girl?"

The smiling face of Edward Corcoran disappeared. He believed his job was to do the right thing for his clients, and he did. This $75,000-a-year district attorney from Vermont had no right to question him or demand anything from him. "I don't know those individuals," he answered. "Well, that's funny," Rocky smirked as he leaned forward in his chair – those old Everett instincts kicking in. "They told me you paid them $1,000 each to put on fake police badges and uniforms that you probably got from a costume shop." Rocky watched the veneer of importance slip from this fixer.

Rocky knew he had the upper hand now. "Yeah, and they told me about a couple of other scams you had them do. You had them pose as IRS agents to some poor slob who lost his hand in an industrial accident. How much did the company pay you to squeeze this guy for a workman's comp settlement? A guy who made a few cash bucks as a bookie and never reported it?"

As Rocky spoke, the stout Ed Corcoran seemed to be retreating in size. Rocky observed him slump further and further into his fancy leather chair. He was actually enjoying watching this son-of-a-bitch squirm.

"Oh, and I guess you really get into this impersonation thing. They also told me you posed as an attorney on that notorious restaurant feud case that went on for years. You remember the one where the two brothers tried to get as much dirt on each other as they could to win the case? I heard you poked around enough to get more dirt for your client than the other side did. You must be really proud of that one, Ed."

Finally, a for-once-in-his-life beaten Ed Corcoran asked, "What do you want? The case is over isn't it?"

Rocky said, "Yeah, from what I gather, you engineered that too. You're quite a guy. What I want is the truth. Why did you do it? If it were your child who was possibly molested, wouldn't you want to know the truth?"

For Edward Corcoran, the truth was the last thing on his mind. Doing the right thing for his clients was his truth. That, and getting paid for all of his creative work.

So Edward Corcoran did what he always did in these situations — he abdicated responsibility. "It was all Dr. Jim Ryan's idea. He had this image as a physician to uphold, and he simply wanted the problem to go away."

Rocky couldn't stop himself. "So that's what the Gomez family was to you – a problem. They weren't flesh and blood, people with hopes and dreams. It didn't matter to you that you sent them to a violent place where gangs cut your arms off. Most importantly, that boy Jon Ryan would not be dead now if you simply did the right thing.

Ed Corcoran defended himself. "I am not responsible for anything. Yes, I probably should not have listened to Dr. Ryan, but there is no blood on my hands."

With that statement, Ed Corcoran seemed to regain his impressed image of himself. "Do your bosses know you are here?" he asked threateningly. "No," Rocky said as he got up from the chair and walked around the desk. Ed knew he had challenged someone he regretted. Rocky's thick body stood over the seated investigator. Ed could not get up if he wanted to. He was forced to listen to the old athlete. "You know what you are, Ed? A crook—a crook who should go to jail. I have put people in jail who have caused less mayhem than you. I don't know how a person like you can live with himself. But unfortunately, you have to have a conscience to think like that."

With that, Rocky turned to leave the office. He did not acknowledge the cheery receptionist when she said, "Have a good day, Mr. Conley." Inside the office, Ed Corcoran composed himself. He dabbed his reddened face, wiping the perspiration from his forehead. He tightened his tie, brushed off his suit, and looked at his impressive image in the mirror. He then made a series of phone calls.

Rocky Conley drove the five hours home in silence. He could not even listen to the radio. He was angry that amoral people like Ed Corcoran existed. He was angry that it was the poor and powerless people who paid the price. That was why he loved sports so much. It didn't matter if you were rich or poor. You supported your teammates, and if you worked hard together, you obtained victory; a victory that was pure and above politics.

Rocky was forced to have an honest dialogue with himself on the ride home. He was getting tired of all the bullshit on the job. All the deals, usually for people who had money. In this wistful state, Rocky thought that he would love to change careers. He would love to be a football coach someday. No bullshit there. Maybe in a couple of years, when I can retire…

Rocky got back to his Vermont office by 3 p.m. He needed to get to work on his domestic violence case that was going to trial soon. He had interviewed the hospitalized woman, who initially did not want to press charges. Rocky had to use all his persuasive skills to convince the woman with the black eye and swollen face to get help. "What's the use?" she had said. "He will just beat me again when he gets out of jail. "Yes," Rocky answered, "And next time he might not stop with you. He might beat your kids, too." The woman then signed her affidavit.

Rocky was working on the case when Colonel Saunders barged into his office. "What the hell did you do to Edward Corcoran?" he demanded. "He's telling everyone you threatened him. And I do mean everyone. He knows a lot of people, Rocky."

Rocky started to answer, but he was interrupted. "You will call this Ed Corcoran and apologize. And then you will drop the case. It's over. Do you understand?" the colonel ordered.

"You don't care what I found out about this guy? He's a piece of shit." "I don't care," said Colonel Saunders. A tense quiet enveloped the office. Rocky thought carefully about his next words. He liked Colonel Saunders personally, but he didn't respect him now. "I can't do that, boss. It's just not right." Rocky then placed his badge on the desk. "I resign," he said, "Take care, Colonel." As he walked away, Rocky ignored the colonel's pleas to come back.

# Chapter 10: Ramon's Revenge

WEEKS AFTER HER BROTHER'S DEATH, Chelsea walked into a decaying fortress for prisoners in Montpelier, Vermont. Since the moment Rocky Conley named Ramon as her brother's killer, Chelsea had vowed to meet him. She had to learn about Jon's final moments. The Chauncey Correctional Institute held her brother's killer, Ramon Gomez, who after a series of telephone conversations had agreed to see her. The facility had been built nearly one hundred years earlier, and looked like a medieval fortress built by a king who had little money left for frills.

The tepid beginning of summer weather seemed to accentuate the odors that Chelsea inhaled as she entered the building. A stench of ammonia combined with stale paint permeated Chelsea's nostrils as she passed the multiple layers of security required for entrance. All the walls were a pale green, and the pale facades of all the correctional officers seemed to melt into one cacophony of lime. Eventually she was deposited behind a glass wall clouded by fingerprints and whatever else people could leave on glass. A 1950s style black telephone was in front of Chelsea, and a nearby guard told her she could talk to Ramon with it when he entered.

Within a few minutes, a prisoner shuffled in. Chelsea had never met Ramon but would have immediately recognized him as Maria's brother. He had the same full mouth and broad nose as his sister, thought Chelsea. His once-swarthy complexion now resembled the colorless visage of everyone here. He did not have the deep laugh lines at the corner of each eye, however, and his somber gaze reflected a person who had no reason to smile. Ramon pointed to the phone, and Chelsea picked it up. She began by thanking Ramon for seeing her. "Maria talked about you so much that I felt I knew you," he told her. An awkward silence followed as each seemed to be sizing up the other one.

Finally, Chelsea asked Ramon how Maria was doing. Ramon sadly shook his head. In clear English he responded, "Terrible." He explained that Maria lived in a small apartment in the capital of San Salvador. " My nephew Roberto has been threatened by one of the violent gangs that prowl the city. My sister worries every day that he will be killed by other gangs, or the police. One day on her way to work in a small restaurant near her apartment, she saw the bodies of two boys Roberto's age in the street. They had been hacked to death rather than shot. Maria and some of the other neighbors stayed with the bodies for hours, unable to touch them or identify them until the police arrived. It was only then, when the bodies were turned over, that Maria had her prayers answered. Roberto was not one of them."

Ramon looked at Chelsea directly and said, "This should not have happened, Chelsea. We had a good life in the United States." Chelsea could not find the words to respond. The comprehension of what her family had done to Maria's was too great for her to endure. She buried her head in her arms and wept.

Ramon helped Chelsea by continuing the conversation. "I remember the night when Maria fell into my arms after she left your home for the last time. Alisa had gone to work with Maria that day, and she said something had happened at the house. At first I thought that your family was upset about something. Maria explained that it involved Jon, but she would not say anything more. We went to Alisa's bedroom and asked Roberto to leave the room. My nephew knew something was wrong with his sister. Alisa had her head under the covers, as if she could not look at her mother. Maria eventually got her daughter to talk. Jon had invited her into his bedroom to play a video game. She said he had a 'funny' look on his face, and he locked the door behind her. It took my sister several tries to get Alisa to tell her what happened. With the covers of her bed drawn tighter, she told us Jon had put his hand down her underwear and "touched" her where she peed. She told us how afraid she had been, and she had tried to leave the room, but Jon pushed her down hard. Then Alisa stopped and would not say anymore."

As Chelsea tried to imagine if her brother was capable of what she was hearing, Ramon revealed more. "We sat up all night talking about what to do. Maria wanted to quit your family's home right away and get another job. She was so afraid that because we are illegal, we all would be deported. In my sister's mind, as terrible as what happened to Alisa was, risking deportation would be worse for her.

Ramon told Chelsea how he had pounded his hands on the table and said that this was not right. He felt they must go to the police. He knew that for years their family had been saving for an immigration attorney to help them get green cards. And given the family's honest, crime-free labor in this country, combined with Alisa's birth in the United States, deportation would not happen. He sobbed angrily, " I was the one who told Maria to go to your father."

Ramon revealed that Maria spoke to Dr. Ryan about Jon the next day, a Friday. Maria said Dr. Ryan reacted calmly and said he would talk to Jon that weekend. Dr. Ryan told Maria to go home and be with her daughter.

Ramon explained that on Saturday, the family received a call from an immigration attorney. He asked if he could see the family the following day. Ramon recalled that they saw a federal officer named Mr. Price. Mr. Price arrived Sunday morning, accompanied by two agents. Flashing badges, the stern agents told the family they had received a report stating that they were here illegally and were to be deported immediately. Alisa and Roberto would be allowed to stay, given their U.S. birth, but Ramon and Maria would have to leave. Maria was told that her children would be in the custody of the state if they remained here. The immigration officials did not want to hear about their proper lifestyle or the fact that they were going to apply for green cards. "This is irrelevant to your illegal status," they declared.

With rapt attention, Chelsea listened as Ramon explained how the agents offered the family "a deal." If everyone, including Ramon, Maria, and her children, agreed to leave immediately for El Salvador, they would help them become legal citizens. Roberto and Alisa were birthright citizens, so they could probably get visas in about six months. The agents further promised to help the family get an apartment in San Salvador, close to the immigration offices. The agents required the decision that night.

Later that night, Ramon and Maria sat at the kitchen table weeping. Alisa and Roberto grew frightened and asked what was wrong. The children begged not to be left in the U.S. without their mother. As Ramon admonished himself for sending Maria to Dr. Ryan, his sister made the decision to leave with the children. "Maybe they will help us get legal." Ramon disagreed and thought they should just leave Boston and go somewhere else in the U.S., perhaps to Florida where they had distant cousins. "I can't be without my kids," countered Maria. By the following Tuesday, Maria and her children were on a plane to San Salvador.

Ramon, however, did not get on the plane. He vacated the apartment, intent on getting "his revenge," and simply disappeared.

Chelsea felt waves of pain as Ramon revealed this history behind the deportation. She mentally pictured her friend Maria contemplating the life-and-death decision forced upon her. The pain increased as Chelsea considered the possibility that her brother had been capable of such an act.

Chelsea asked Ramon if she could talk to him about her brother's murder. Ramon said that when his sister left, he blamed himself for his family's demise. "I failed everyone – my brother Luis, my parents, who died of broken hearts, and now my sister Maria and her children." Ramon sobbed, "My failure turned into poisonous anger at the one person who caused all these evils: Jon."

Ramon revealed to Chelsea that he decided he did not want to live any longer. When he heard from Maria how terrible life was in San Salvador, his grief worsened. There were many gangs demanding money or ransom simply for walking on the street. Maria reported that the immigration authorities in San Salvador knew nothing about her case. They told her to hire an attorney, or it might take years for her to get a green card.

Ramon found himself going to Wellesley and staring at the Ryan home, growing more and more angry. "One day I even saw you laughing with your mom as you walked outside, and seeing such happiness made me mad at you." Chelsea pondered the injustice of one family being so happy and another being torn apart.

"One day, on one of these trips to Wellesley, I saw a local paper with a picture of your dad and brother . Below the smiling father and son, the article revealed that Jon was a freshman basketball star at Winchester College in

Vermont. It was then that I decided to wipe that smile off your brother's face. The next thing I knew, I was buying a gun from my co-worker in the city."

"Do you want me to tell you the rest, Chelsea?"

"Yes, Ramon. I want to know everything."

Ramon continued explaining that shortly after seeing the article, he packed a tent with some clothing and food, and then traveled to Winchester College. He walked that campus numerous times and got a sense of Jon's routine, especially around the gymnasium. One day, on a poster at the library, he saw that the basketball team had an away game on a Friday night. Since he didn't really care if he got caught, Ramon decided to shoot Jon, even if some teammates were around.

So that Friday, when the bus returned to the gymnasium, Ramon was hiding in the shrubs. He heard Jon shout to his roommates, "I have to go back to my locker. See you in a few minutes." It was a golden opportunity, but Ramon felt neither lucky nor unlucky as he awaited Jon's reemergence from the gym. He surprised Jon, and with an unsteady aim shot him in the leg. "I hadn't been prepared to say anything to Jon, but as I moved closer to him, I said, 'This is for Alisa.' Then I shot him in the head."

Chelsea's head dropped into her lap as Ramon uttered these words. She now knew how her brother had spent the last moments of his life. She had one last question for Ramon. "Did my brother say anything to you?" Ramon bowed his head and answered, "No."

Chelsea left the prison with only one goal in mind. She must secure Maria's return to the United States. Before she did that, however, she was going to have a chat with Ed Corcoran, the investigator her dad had hired to fix things: the man who had tricked Maria into returning to El Salvador.

# Chapter 11: Private Investigator Edward Corcoran

IF THE F.B.I. HAD A PICTURE of the classic F.B.I. agent in the dictionary, Edward "Ed" Corcoran's picture would appear. Tall and handsome, with a gray crew cut atop a long, lean face and a square jaw, Ed had narrow, deep-set gray eyes that grew dark when angry and rarely danced with any glee. Ed was all business, and although they had never met, J. Edgar Hoover would have liked the image. That's why it was a surprise when, in mid-career with the F.B.I., Ed retired from the agency. His friends soon learned not to ask him about that. His dark eyes told them not to probe further.

Leaving the F.B.I. was the best thing that happened to Ed Corcoran's career, however. He formed Corcoran and Associates, one of the largest private investigation firms in

Boston. But few knew that. Ed liked to "fly under the radar,, so to speak, and for him publicity was bad. His success came from word-of-mouth from satisfied clients. For twenty years, he never had to recruit business. His staff of investigators examined anything from wayward husbands to false workmens' compensation claims.

Ed Corcoran saw himself as a "fixer" rather than a private investigator. He considered himself a highly moral man who insisted his three teenage children accompany him and his wife to church on Sunday. While Ed had strong feelings about capital punishment and abortion, these feelings were malleable when it came to business.

Ed Corcoran approached his profession with a zeal that some compared to a starving dog gnawing on a bone. When a client paid Ed a $400 an hour fee, his services came with a unique passion. He spent considerable time understanding the perspective of a client - to a point where Ed was capable of some internal mental juggling that allowed him to justify his client's position without regret. Ed could somehow convince himself that his client was always right.

He recalled one divorce case with a special pride. The husband, whom Ed was representing, had been forced out of his home due to a bogus domestic violence charge. The man wanted custody of his three young children. His divorce attorney contacted Ed, the best investigator he knew, to get some dirt on the mother.

Ed learned from the husband that early in the marriage the couple shared an opiate problem. On two or three occasions the wife, who was a nurse, took some of her patients' unused opiates home. Fortunately, the couple had overcome their mutual problem.

Ed used this information to help the dad get principal custody of the children. Although the wife had an unblemished career as an operating room nurse, she feared losing her career. She agreed to the custody arrangement. The fact that his client may have been an abuser, or that the children would be better off with the mom, did not concern Ed Corcoran. In his mind he had done the right thing. His sound client deserved custody of his children.

One day Ed was in his office, chatting business with his colleagues, when his secretary buzzed him to say that a Chelsea Ryan was in her office wanting to speak with him. The secretary added that she was Dr. Jim Ryan's daughter.

A bit perplexed, Ed asked if her dad was with her. The secretary replied that Chelsea was alone. As Ed considered whether he should see her, he recalled Dr. Ryan's case with great satisfaction. Rocky Conley's visit had not caused Ed any doubt that he had done a great job for his client. Ed had met Dr. Ryan during a legal case which occurred at the hospital when Dr. Ryan was in charge. A nurse had accused a renowned cardiologist at the hospital of persistent sexual advances. It culminated, she alleged, in a groping incident by the doctor in a changing room after heart surgery. After threatening to expose some past indiscretions he had dug up about her, Ed negotiated a quiet settlement, and the nurse relocated to another hospital. Ed was not troubled that this was the third such incident involving this cardiologist.

When Dr. Ryan hired Ed to help with Jon's troubles, Ed remembered that his biggest challenge was with the doctor himself. Dr. Ryan was obsessed with the molestation accusations and what he considered the difficulty of negating them.

He recalled Dr. Ryan, head in hands, saying that his son could never have done such a thing.

To Ed Corcoran, the case was simple. Maria Gomez was here illegally, and that made the case without merit. Somehow Ed's logic escaped the fact that the accuser, Alisa, was an American citizen by birth. In Ed Corcoran's mind, this foreign family had no right to destroy Dr. Ryan's family.

Ed was convinced that he could handle the logistics of having his investigators impersonate immigration officials. He would make them so believable in uniform and paperwork that the Gomez family would run, not walk, onto the first airplane to El Salvador.

No, Ed's problem was Dr. Ryan. The doctor worried about the legality of the plan. He worried about Maria and her family. It took Ed Corcoran all his twisted passion to convince Dr. Ryan to agree to his scheme. Dr. Ryan finally agreed to the plan, with the condition that they obtain an apartment for the family in San Salvador, and she would receive $300 each month, which Dr. Ryan would pay. Some of Ed's contacts put him in touch with Oscar Cruz, who took care of the logistics in San Salvador. Ed recalled with a smile that what convinced Dr. Ryan to finally go along with the plan was his concern for Maria. Ed told the doctor that if Maria ever wanted to become an American citizen, she would have to return to

El Salvador and apply for a visa. Ed said, "This case is not about your son."

Meanwhile, an angry Chelsea sat in Ed Corcoran's office for two hours. Since Chelsea had heard this man's name from her dad, she had wanted to meet him — and not only to confront him. Perhaps Mr. Corcoran's talents could also be used to rescue Maria when he learned the horror he had engineered. Chelsea told the secretary she was not leaving without seeing Mr. Corcoran, even if she did not have an appointment. Finally, Ed Corcoran appeared before her, his narrow eyes absorbing the young woman. He invited Chelsea into his impressive office overlooking Boston Harbor and its bobbing boats.

Chelsea demanded to know if his office was in any way responsible for the fake deportation of the Gomez family. She then explained that she had recently visited the office of immigration attorney Max Roosevelt. The attorney had told her that a ruse of some sort had been concocted against Maria and her family. Ed Corcoran calmly asked, "Why are you asking me?"

Unknown to Ed, Chelsea had done some investigative work that would make him proud. Following the meeting with Mr. Roosevelt, Chelsea had contacted Maria in San

Salvador. She asked Maria who set up the bank account. Maria explained that her landlord, Oscar Cruz, had taken her to a local bank to open an account. Maria knew nothing else except that the first of each month, $300 appeared in the account—money that was literally lifesaving to her family.

Chelsea got Maria's landlord Oscar Cruz's telephone number and telephoned him. He identified himself in broken English. As soon as Chelsea mentioned the name Ryan, Mr. Cruz hung up. Repeated calls to Mr. Cruz went unanswered.

Chelsea pursued another route and contacted the Bank of El Salvador, where the money was wired each month. She wanted to know who wired the money. She reached a bank vice president who spoke English and she shared her purpose. Immediately, the bank official reverted to Spanish and responded, "Yo no hablo ingles." A frustrated Chelsea received the same response when she contacted anyone associated with the bank.

An exasperated Chelsea went to see attorney Max Roosevelt. Twirling his mustache, Max said, "Two can play at this game." He prepared an impressive subpoena with all types of Federal sanctions for the Bank of El Salvador if it did not cooperate. Meanwhile,

Max recognized that he had no legal right to this information in a foreign country. He was bluffing, and it paid off – the bank caved. Chelsea was given the name of Edward Corcoran and Associates as the source of the deposit.

Now Ed Corcoran understood that the young lady had traced the money back to his office. Chelsea asked, "Did my father put you up to this?" Ed Corcoran never liked his back against the wall. "Maybe you should ask him," was his response. "I did, and all he would say is that Jon is not guilty of anything."

Ed narrowed his dark eyes further, "Look, I always believe anyone I'm talking to is wired or using a recorder." Chelsea looked surprised, "Of course not," she said as she opened up her purse and immodestly lifted her blouse. "I just want the truth."

Ed continued, "So long as we understand each other. I am only talking in hypotheticals here. If someone did deport this family, it was only right – they were illegal." Chelsea corrected him, "The children were legal. You deported their mother and father, and the children would never stay without them." Ed responded calmly, "Then they should obtain citizenship like every other foreigner who wants to live in this great country." ................

Chelsea felt her face redden with rage. "There is no more 'they.' Carlos Gomez died in El Salvador." But Ed did not miss a beat: "They should have come here legally."

Chelsea stood up, "Do you know the pain you caused this family? Their lives are all in jeopardy from the pain you caused." Ed Corcoran had heard enough. "You better talk to your dad — and again, speaking in the hypothetical here, your dad might be in trouble if what you are saying is true. Are you prepared to wreck your dad's career, young lady?" Speechless, Chelsea turned and stormed out of the office. She thought to herself that this man had the morals of the devil.

Later that night, Ed Corcoran enjoyed a nice dinner with his wife and another couple. The Ryan and the Gomez family did not enter his compartmentalized mind at all.

# Chapter 12: Helene is Reborn

HELENE RYAN SAT ALONE in the office of Dr. Lidia Greene and reflected on her journey with this psychologist. Jon had been dead for two months when Helene realized she needed help. The sleeping pills her husband had prescribed did not help during her waking hours. She had begged her husband to join her in therapy, but he refused. He seemed to deal with his grief by working exhaustive hours at the hospital. Dr. and Mrs. Ryan were now living like two grief-stricken ghosts, physically close but emotionally invisible to each other.

During the initial therapy sessions, Dr. Greene listened while Helene blamed herself for Jon's death. Helene attributed his death to her passiveness when Alisa's allegations were first made. "I should have talked to Maria" became "I should have talked to Jon." And then finally, "I should have told my husband, no, you won't take care of it your way!" Dr. Greene simply allowed her to feel comfortable sharing her emotions during those early sessions, while the therapist reassured her patient that she did not cause Jon's death.

In painstaking therapy that grew to three sessions per week, Dr. Greene helped peel away at the amalgam of Helene's decades of buried emotions. Each layer of sadness, anger, and even joy had meaning for Helene that Dr. Greene helped her to confront. This was difficult for Helene, who was a champion denier. She had buried a lifetime of fears, disappointments, and trauma by minimizing their impact on her life. Helene came to understand that her focus on looking good, shopping, and even drinking were superficial attempts to hide her pain. By the spring after Jon's death, she came to believe what Dr. Greene fostered in her. She now had the desire and courage to confront herself, to uncover her true identity, and to focus on her wants and needs for the future.

The grief that initially brought Helene to Dr. Greene expanded to all the unresolved grief of her past. Helene grew up outside of Hartford, Connecticut. She was the oldest child, and the first generation child of Italian parents who had emigrated from the small village of Cirino outside of Naples in southern Italy. Her father was a bricklayer who brought his considerable skills to America. He eventually built a successful masonry business, which her two younger brothers ran today. Her mother was a typical Italian who had her dad's pasta ready every night sharply at 6 p.m. Helene and her two brothers were expected to be at the table on time. Her tired dad did not have to refill his wine during dinner, so her mom dutifully did this. An Italian mom from the "old country" who had simple needs, Helene's mom's true pleasure was seeing her pasta-filled family members laughing at the table. Helene recalled that both her brothers came to expect her mother, or their sister, to refill their milk glasses or jump up and get them whatever they needed. She learned quickly that women were subservient to men.

As a child, Helene looked at her mother's role in the family as one she should adopt. Be quiet and content, with a nice home and a husband who was a good provider. Since her parents were not proficient in English, they relied on Helene, especially as she got older, to communicate with the outside world. While her dad struggled with broken English, her mom spoke almost entirely Italian. By the seventh grade, Helene was communicating with repairmen and paying the property taxes on the family home. She often felt like a little parent in the home.

When she reached adolescence, Helene often wished she had an older sister to give her guidance. Until then, the "old world" ways of her home did not conflict with the world outside her home. Until then, her mom bought all of Helene's clothes, and cosmetics were never even mentioned.

In middle school, however, this comfortable feeling collided with the frenzy that is female adolescence. Shy and reserved Helene listened to her popular classmates swear, discuss the best belly rings, and talk about their boyfriends. The situation was complicated by Helene's blossoming body, which drew the attention of both boys and jealous girls alike. Helene resolved all this inner anguish by being sweet and nice, and rarely sharing her true feelings with anyone.

By high school, the increasingly popular Helene was actually the envy of other students. She absorbed the art of applying makeup and had a flair for contemporary fashion that accentuated her slim but developing figure. She was also an excellent student. Although she sweated profusely before every exam, she aced them all. Her goal was to be the class valedictorian and get a scholarship to college.

These changes in Helene did not go unnoticed in her traditional home. While her mom was proud of her beautiful daughter, she did not approve of her clothes or makeup. Helene could not share with her the pressures of being a high school female in America. Helene's mom constantly told her daughter that she was beautiful without all that "mud" on her face.

In his patriarchal world, Helene's dad simply did not connect with this "American daughter." He did not consider good grades important, particularly for a daughter. He thought Helene should get married out of high school. In fact, one of his masonry workers had a son in Italy who wanted to come to America and marry her. Helene was astounded that her father actually believed it was a good idea as he showed her a photo of the young Italian man. Additionally, her dad made it clear that he would not pay for college for a daughter. Helene felt more and more pressure to achieve in order to get a scholarship.

Helene rarely confided in her parents—for that matter, she rarely shared herself with anyone. From the outside, teachers and friends thought her sweet and successful. But inside,

Helene's stomach was turning with anger and anxiety. The one thing she could control was her food intake. Always a picky eater, by senior year Helene was borderline bulimic.

Her eating issues remained a part of her life throughout college and her marriage. It was in therapy with Dr. Greene that she first discovered her underlying need to control something – anything - in her case, eating.

Helene's passiveness was challenged by her dad's behavior in her senior year. She dated rarely, and in fact chose not to attend her junior or senior prom. No need for dates to step into her traditional Italian home of wedding cookies and anisette.

After much convincing by her friends, one night she dressed for a homecoming event. She decided to wear a tight, stylish mini-dress that accentuated her figure. Her father called her a "Puttana" (whore) and demanded she change her dress. Helene raced to her room and cried her eyes out. No one came to console her. She did not go to the homecoming event. Rather, she promised herself that she would work even harder to get a scholarship and become the class valedictorian.

Neck-and-neck with another classmate for a scholarship, Helene existed on coffee for much of her senior year. She had little time to sleep as she studied relentlessly. Her competition was the daughter of a prominent physician. Helene felt that this girl did not even need a scholarship, but naturally this underlying feeling of anger was buried within her.

With the help of supportive teachers, many of whom knew of her family difficulties, Helene was chosen as class valedictorian. Her acceptance to Remington University in Boston came with a full academic scholarship. She was ecstatic. She could now free herself from Old World shackles and pursue her occupational dream – to become an attorney. She envisioned herself as an advocate for the needy.

Through therapy, Dr. Greene helped Helene to see that this need for advocacy represented herself as the little girl who had no one to advocate for her.

College initially met all of the dreams that Helene had envisioned. Surrounded by eager freshman students who grew up much differently than she did, Helene quickly adapted to the college culture. Weekdays were for classes and studies, and weekends were for football games and parties.

Helene loved the academic rigor of college. Unlike her free-spirited roommate Nancy, who often blew off morning classes after a late night, Helene was often the first person in class. She grew to love the stimulating debates in her law classes. She grew more and more confident in herself, eventually becoming captain of the freshman debate team. She could envision herself arguing case law one day in a courtroom as she debated other students.

Helene received a 4.0 in her fall semester at Remington and a nearly identical 3.8 in the spring semester. The year seemed to fly by. Helene had never been happier in her life and formed a tight circle of friends on campus. She was growing confident in her abilities, and her high grades ensured that her scholarship would extend until senior year.

Going home the summer after her freshman year was difficult. The Old World customs in her home grated on her. Her dad's attitude about women conflicted with all the opportunities for women outside the home. As quickly as possible, Helene secured a summer clerical job at the college. She was allowed to live on campus and only returned home infrequently.

Sophomore year found an excited Helene taking six courses. She loved the stimulating environment of her classes. She would have taken even more electives, if allowed to, but her advisor strongly rejected it. She had a new roommate, Diane, who reminded Helene of herself. Diane appeared quiet and pleasing, but Helene saw that she had serious ambition beneath the façade. "I'll help her come out of her shell," thought Helene.

Little did Helene know that it was herself who would need help. In her political science class, Helene found herself next to a large bear of a man named Sean. Helene recognized him from the football team. He was so thick, he barely fit into his seat. He turned to Helene as he struggled to get comfortable and commented, "They have got to made these desks bigger." He had an easy smile in that burly body that exuded thickness combined with muscle.

Helene found Sean easy to talk to, and she began to linger after class more and more to chat with him. In early October, he invited her to a party at his fraternity house. Sean said that it was Homecoming weekend, and after their football victory on Saturday, it would be the best party on campus.

Helene had heard of the wild parties at the fraternity house. Students had to be invited by someone to get in, and it was always the popular ones who got to go. Helene hesitated at first, having been previously warned about this fraternity's reputation, but Sean's easygoing smile convinced her.

As Helene got dressed for the party, she had to admit to herself that the new strapless silver dress which accentuated her shapely figure looked great on her. As she arrived at the fraternity house, she saw that the party was in full swing, especially since Remington had defeated their arch-rival Perry University. Two beefy-looking athletes appraised her up and down and asked who invited her. With the mention of Sean's name, both opened their hands like a stout drawbridge and ushered her in.

Sean greeted Helene with drinks in both hands. The atmosphere was crazed – wall to wall people, music pounding, and alcohol-infused voices holding increasingly incoherent conversations. Helene coughed as she tasted her pint-sized drink that seemed to be all alcohol.

Sean's easy laugh and the atmosphere in the room finally got Helene to relax. Before she knew it, Sean returned with another pint-sized drink. Helene found that the second one seemed to go down easier. Soon, the loud music and crush of humanity around her weakened her legs. With nowhere to sit, Sean suggested they go upstairs to his room. Helene agreed.

No sooner had Helene sat than Sean started kissing her. Starting to feel nauseous, Helene said she wanted to go home. Sean got more and more aggressive, telling her to stay with him. Before she could comprehend what was happening, Sean pushed Helene onto the bed. Two hundred and fifty pounds of bulk squeezed the air out of her lungs. He ripped off her panties as she weakly repeated, "No," over and over. But Sean forced himself into her, yelling, "You want it, bitch." When it was over, Sean sat beside her wordlessly with a look of contempt on his face. He left her in the room. Barely comprehending what had happened to her, Helene looked in the mirror. She saw eyeliner streaking down her face, and her dress ripped nearly in two. Helene grabbed a football jacket out of the closet and ran downstairs. She felt all the eyes that were on her as she ran out the door. No one said a word to her.

Helene replayed the events of that night over and over. She had been alone, physically and emotionally. She told no one, and she never considered reporting the rape to the police, or even getting counseling. Eventually, however, she could no longer attend classes. The voices of low self-esteem in her head were getting louder. After the spring semester of her sophomore year, she returned to her parents' home. Her grades had dropped precipitously and her scholarship was at risk. She worked at a local bakery that summer and did not return to college in the fall. Her parents never asked why.

Her father managed to secure her an administrative job at Hartford Hospital. His masonry work on the hospital's administrator's home had one perk for her. In her administrative position, she crossed paths with Dr. Ryan, who was a young intern. Enthralled by her beauty, the young doctor pressured her to marry him after their third date. Ensconced in a serious relationship for the first time, and in a fragile mental state, Helene accepted.

Helene now realized the seeds of the later Ryan family dysfunction occurred with this acceptance. "I loved my husband, but only as much as someone who did not love herself was able." She now painfully realized that she'd transferred all of her repressed memories onto Chelsea. "All the focus on not getting married – the focus on looks and clothes – was about me. I was so full of denial, I didn't know my own child. I failed my daughter." She told Dr. Greene her many regrets. "I should have gotten counseling before I said yes to marriage. Jon would be alive today if I did. Today, I would have taken Jon to the police station myself." Dr. Greene understood her patient's mental torture and had to help Helene forgive herself.

For all of Helene's growth in therapy, there was one thing she could not share with Dr. Greene. At the end of each session, the therapist asked if Helene wanted to discuss anything else. Although always tempted, Helene simply could not force the words from her lips. It was much too painful.

After many sessions with Dr. Greene, Helene finally answered "Yes" to the doctor's invitation to share something else. Helene confessed, "I once told my son that I wished he was never born." As soon as she spoke these words, Helene broke down and sobbed uncontrollably on Dr. Greene's couch.

Mountains of used tissues lay at Helene's feet as she revealed her deepest secret. Dr. Greene concluded that this revelation was more painful to Helene than her rape in college. Helene continued, "You see, I didn't want another baby. I knew something was sick inside me. After Chelsea, I wanted to go into counseling. I wasn't even sure I wanted to stay married."

"But my husband constantly begged me to have another child. All he ever said was that he wanted a son. He would ask me again and again to please have just one more child. Then he promised that even if it was a girl, he would be fine with that. I felt so sorry for him that I finally just gave in."

Unlike her pregnancy with Chelsea, Helene's pregnancy with Jon was difficult. She was constantly nauseous. Eight weeks before the birth, she started spotting. Dr. Ryan ordered her to bed and paid housekeepers to care for her. "I often wonder if, in those eight weeks, my son could feel my resentment," Helene said as she wiped her eyes.

"When Jon was born, my husband was on top of the world," reminisced Helene. "All he could talk about was his son; Jon this and Jon that. I'm not sure he even remembered he had a daughter."

"I will admit, Jon was the most beautiful baby I had ever seen. Yet he was a difficult baby. He got his days and nights mixed up. I was so exhausted." A tired Helene often felt guilty because she just did not have the energy for a neglected two-year-old Chelsea.

Helene saw immediate signs that Jon was a far different baby than Chelsea. "Chelsea would play with her dolls by herself for hours. But

Jon needed constant attention. When he spoke, his first word was "No!" Helene smiled and said, "I know that's common for babies, but when Jon said no, he meant it. He would never eat or sleep when you wanted him to."

As Jon grew, Helene saw signs in her son that told her something was wrong. "He was aggressive with other kids. Many of his playdates with preschool classmates ended badly. He even slapped Chelsea when he was angry."

"I spoke to my husband about Jon's behavior. He dismissed my concerns. He would say, 'He's just a boy, it's nothing.' And then he would change the subject and brag about how smart Jon was."

While Dr. Ryan obviously loved Chelsea, he constantly looked for his son when he got home. Helene laughed, "It reminded me of the Godfather movie – the Don was always looking for only one child, his son Michael."

As Jon matured, people seemed to rave about him. Helene commented, "Even my father said he looked like a handsome Italian Count. Everyone, even Jon's teachers, seemed to fawn over his good looks and intelligence; to the point that when he locked a classmate in the closet, no one took it very seriously. People just accepted Jon's excuse that it was only a prank. Naturally, my husband thought the whole thing was overblown."

"But I did not agree with my husband. I identified with that tormented girl who had been locked in the closet." In a loud, angry voice, Helene said, "I wanted to take Jon to counseling then, but my husband overruled me." Helene then said that she saw a dysfunctional family dynamic emerging, but she felt powerless to stop it. My husband and my son became more like buddies, with my husband overlooking and excusing all of Jon's troublesome actions."

In her revelations, Helene finally got to the day in question when she uttered her infamous words. "One day when I picked Jon up at school, I saw a helpless kitten that melted my heart. I probably felt a kinship there, right?" Dr. Greene smiled and said, "Continue, please." "Well, as I carried the kitten into the car, I saw a look in Jon's eyes that only a mother could recognize. My son had a type of cold stare when something unpleasant was happening to him. I saw that look that day, but I put it out of my mind."....................................

"As the days went on, my son let it be known that he hated my kitten. He would ask his father to get rid of it. Dr. Greene, I know he tried to kill the cat!" Helene went on to explain how she came home to see the trembling kitten, soaking wet near a bucket of water. "In a rage, I told my son I wish he was never born. And you see now, Dr. Greene, that this was true. How can I forgive myself?"

Helene went on. "After Jon's wicked act, I knew he needed help, and for once I put my foot down. I insisted that my husband take Jon to a therapist. My husband reluctantly agreed and chose a colleague at the hospital, a psychiatrist. I have never seen my son so angry as on the day we took him to his first session. He had a look of hate directed only at me."

Jon attended three sessions of therapy and then begged his father to allow him to stop. My husband conceded, and Jon's therapy ended. Again, I allowed my husband to overrule me." Dr. Greene said softly, "I bet your husband regrets this now." And then she added, "Helene, you must recognize that all your actions prove that you loved your son."

Her last secret out, Helene spent the next weeks in therapy, largely learning to forgive herself. While some of Helene's guilt was warranted, in Dr. Greene's opinion, most of it was unwarranted. In the past, this guilt prevented Helene from fully developing as a person. The past pacification of guilt – by shopping or focusing on good looks – was now not needed. Dr. Greene saw a growth in Helene's personality developing before her eyes. Helene now talked about a future where she could fulfill professional dreams that had been buried in family pain.

It was Dr. Greene's suggestion that they bring in Chelsea for a session. The last guilt-induced hurdle for Helene was rediscovering her adult daughter. Dr. Greene felt this was the most important hurdle. There was no way for Helene to get help for Jon now. But she could restructure a relationship with the most important person in her life – her daughter.

Chelsea was a bit wary about attending the counseling session. She had resisted efforts by her mother to get her own counseling. All Chelsea cared about was trying to help Maria and her family get back to America. She had little desire to sit around talking to someone about her sadness. But she needed to do something.

If Chelsea were honest, curiosity was the primary reason she agreed to go to the session. She wondered how someone could change as much as her mother had in recent weeks. Chelsea initially thought it was Jon's death that brought them closer. She slowly realized her mom was changing. Helene had never spent as much time asking what Chelsea thought about things. During their shopping trips when Chelsea was a young girl, her mom's comments were always critical. "You have to dress better, Chelsea." These comments only made Chelsea's weak self-esteem grow weaker. Now mother-and-daughter shopping trips were very relaxed and positive. "You look great, Chelsea. But I just can't understand how you kids pay for pants with holes in them."

Helene inquired about Chelsea's passions. "Are you sure you want to be a nurse? Reach for your highest goals. You are capable of anything, Chelsea."

Chelsea attended the session, and many more. She learned so much she hadn't known about her mother. She now saw her mother as a young, ambitious girl growing up in a patriarchal home—a home that did not honor women—with a father who called his own daughter a "whore." She admired her mother as a daughter who overcame this.

As a child, Chelsea heard her dad proudly proclaim at the dinner table that Helene had been class valedictorian. Chelsea had never understood her mother's embarrassed reaction. Now she understood.

Helene recounted to her daughter how all her dreams were destroyed the night of her rape.

"It changed me, Chelsea. I never looked at the world the same." Helene then took her daughter's hands and said, "It also affected me as a mother, Chelsea. I used you to cover up all my fears. That's why I was always lecturing you about dating and finding the right person. My biggest regret, Chelsea, is that with all my pain, I was not there for you. I never could enjoy the daughter I love more than anything in this world."

The sessions then turned to the painful topic of Jon. "Dr. Greene has helped me to forgive myself, Chelsea." She revealed to Chelsea the infamous line she had yelled at Jon. Chelsea had never heard of the incident with the kitten, and as a lover of animals, it horrified her. It forced Chelsea to reexamine her whole life with her brother.

Unlike Helene, Chelsea knew the details of the "wedgie" incident with Roberto. In fact, Maria had discussed with her several incidents whereby Jon had hurt Roberto. Once Maria had shown her a bruise on her son's arm. Maria told her that Jon hit Roberto because he had "touched" his Legos without permission.

"I had never seen Maria as mad as she was that day," Chelsea said as she relayed to Dr. Greene and her mom the "wedgie" incident. Jon had taken Roberto to the nearby playground.

There, he saw several friends from school. With Jon's encouragement, the boys proceeded to taunt Roberto about his brown skin. Embarrassed, Roberto played alone on the tire swing. The group of boys snuck up behind him and tried to pull his underwear up over his head.

When her son told her about what the boys did, Maria tried to talk to Jon, but he denied it ever happened. Maria never allowed Roberto to come to the Ryan home again. "Now that I think about it," Helene said, "Maria never wanted to bring Alisa to our house. She only brought her on rare occasions when no one else could watch her." As it dawned on the three ladies, Chelsea opined, "Do you think Maria had a premonition?"

As Chelsea was piecing these events together, she saw Jon's behavior in a new light. Did everyone dismiss his disturbing actions until it was too late?

It was in this mental recalculation that Chelsea remembered a long-forgotten incident. Chelsea said to her mother and Dr. Greene, "One day, Maria came into my room laughing. She told me my underwear found itself in Jon's drawer. I never even thought twice about it, even though I noticed that some of my underwear was missing. Is it possible Jon took them?"

Mother and daughter turned nervously to Dr. Greene. Dr. Greene commented, "We will never know if Jon took the underwear. I will say that some character disorders often have sexual components. I know you are looking for clues that explain Jon's behavior. Unfortunately, we may never know the real truth."

With that, therapy sessions with both Chelsea and her mother ended. Chelsea felt closer to her mom now than at any other time in her life. Yes, she had lost a brother, but she'd found a loving mother. This emotional bond united them in a mission – return the Gomez family to America.

# Chapter 13: Max, the Immigration Lawyer

CHELSEA AND HELENE SAT NERVOUSLY in the Boston office of attorney Max Roosevelt. ("Yes, we are related somewhere.") His office was adorned with legal citations and photos of him with families. He had been recommended to the Ryans as a specialist in immigration cases similar to Maria's. These so-called "birthright" cases involve undocumented parents whose children were born in the United States, and therefore were citizens.

Neither Chelsea nor Helene was prepared for the blur of human energy that was Max Roosevelt. ("Call me Max.") Their heads were spinning as Max apologized for his tardiness while dropping files and yelling at his secretary to accept any call from the Honduras Consulate. Chelsea thought he did not look the part of a distinguished attorney with a tailored suit and leather briefcase. He had long hair tied in a ponytail, and wore an untucked shirt and jeans. He was short, with a slight belly that protruded over his pants, but his most distinguishing feature was a flourishing handlebar mustache. As he talked, that mustache roamed all over his face. When his secretary called to him that the Consulate was on the phone, he excused himself. Helene whispered to her daughter, "He looks like a hippie."

It was now May 2009, and Chelsea's admiration for her mom grew each day. It had been Helene's idea to hire an immigration attorney to help Maria. Chelsea's parents were now officially divorced. They had separated in January, largely due to Dr. Ryan's refusal to participate in therapy with his wife. The ease of the settlement reflected more that neither sad spouse had the energy to litigate a divorce. While Helene had probably left "some money on the table," her attorney had negotiated a settlement that met her immediate financial needs. It assured that she could also pay for law school, which she planned to start in the fall. Mother and daughter shared an apartment in Boston.

Chelsea remained on leave from her college. She realized she could not study, since her mind was tormented by the "what-ifs." What if Alisa was wrong about Jon's intentions that day, and it was all a misunderstanding? What if it were actually true? Maybe Jon could have gotten therapy for his character flaw, and he could still be alive. What if her dad had not helped to exile Maria and her family?

While Chelsea's admiration for her mom grew, she could barely speak to her father. Since Jon's death, he had refused to discuss his role in Maria and her family's deportation. He showed little interest in Ramon's conviction, unable or unwilling to address the tragic dominos that he'd created.

The bundle of energy that was Max reentered the room, intruding on Chelsea's thoughts. "Ladies, you mentioned that you needed help securing a visa for someone who was deported?" In painful detail, mother and daughter recounted the circumstances of Jon's death and the relationship to Maria's departure. Helene stated that her husband never acknowledged his role with the immigration authorities, other than commenting that "the problem is going away."

As the ladies spoke, Max quietly took notes. Following their remarks, he leaned back in his chair and offered his legal observations. "Many people believe undocumented parents like Maria have a right to stay in this country if their children are born here. That is not true. Although their children are U.S. citizens, the parents are subject to deportation. I have seen such children put in foster homes or even put up for adoption. When these children turn twenty-one, they can petition for a permanent visa or green card for their parents." He laughed, "We cannot wait that long."

Max continued, "In cases such as Maria's where she was here illegally, she would normally have to remain out of the country for ten years before she could petition for a visa." Watching the women absorb this bad prognosis, Max then offered some hope for Maria. "I have never in all my years in this work seen someone deported in two days. At the very least, Maria was entitled to a hearing with immigration officials, which can take up to several weeks to schedule. In addition, there are 'hardship' waivers that the courts could have considered when the party's safety is at risk. Given the climate in El Salvador, she may well receive an emergency visa."

Max told the Ryans to give him a few days to obtain the legal record of Maria's deportation. Chelsea left the office more hopeful, and no longer concerned about Max's appearance.

After the Ryans left, Max recalled the prominent murder of Jon Ryan. It was such an unusual case that initially captured the public's interest, but seemed to abruptly disappear. Little did he think that this work would draw him into this tragic case.

Unlike many of Max's clients, the Ryans could afford his services. One benefit of his privileged name was that he could choose to do the type of legal work he wanted. A family trust fund relieved him from financial worries. Max recalled how, fresh out of college and working at a prestigious law firm, he spent a weekend dividing the pots and pans of a bitter, divorcing couple. He vowed then that he would do legal work that made a difference. He quickly fell into immigration law, and he treasured those happy photos of clients he had helped, which decorated his office wall. Many of Max's clients were poor people who would give him their last quarters and dollars to reunite their families. And Max routinely did many of these cases pro bono, which his colleagues thought was insane.

In all his years of immigration work, Max had never seen a case like the Gomez case. There was simply no record of the family's deportation. Max called a friendly immigration official, who told Max that the immigration office had no record of involvement with the Gomez family. As far as the officials were concerned, the Gomez family was off their radar.

Could it be possible that the official-looking people who came to the Gomez home were really not immigration workers, but frauds? Max was slowly coming to this conclusion, given the expediency of departure.

In addition, Max recalled that Ramon told Chelsea that his sister was relocated to an apartment in San Salvador. While the deported are often put in shelters in the incoming country, he had never seen immigration secure a private apartment for a family.

Max tried to contact Dr. Ryan, but he refused to call the lawyer back. Max then began a series of phone conversations with Maria in El Salvador. She confirmed the facts of the quick trip out of the country, and the acquiring of the apartment which was leased for her. His suspicions about the false exile were supported by the mysterious deposit of $300 into Maria's account each month. He had a legal colleague in San Salvador interview Maria and prepare affidavits. The affidavits and a hardship petition were then filed in the Consulate Office in El Salvador.

Max decided that, rather than engaging in a legal battle of subpoenas with Dr. Ryan, he would pursue a hardship visa for Maria. Hardship visas take into account the safety of the deported family, which was certainly an issue in El Salvador. In addition, the fact that Maria's family was self-supporting and without any criminal activity was a further positive in Max's mind. With the help of her attorney in El Salvador, Maria documented the violence surrounding her each day. By affidavit, she wrote that Alisa had recently been abducted, and only released when Roberto agreed to join the same gang that had abducted his sister.

On September 1, 2009, Attorney Roosevelt was on the first flight out of Boston to El Salvador. He would need time to build his case on behalf of Maria.

# Chapter 14: The Trial

ATTORNEY MAX ROOSEVELT WAS GREETED at the San Salvador airport by his colleague Attorney Elena Sanchez. Although they consulted on several other immigration cases, they had never met in person. Attorney Sanchez had always impressed Max by her competence. He never had to worry about the thoroughness of her pleadings or the timeliness in filing petitions. The forty-something Max had to admit that Attorney Sanchez was also impressive to his eyes. Tall and mocha-skinned, the stylish woman greeted Max with a warm smile and handshake. Max took a quick glance at her ringless left hand as he self-consciously wiped the sweat off his unruly mustache. He was delighted to hear Elena ask if he wanted to get something to eat.

The couple sat in one of the outdoor cafes that lined the side streets of the capital city of El

Salvador. Elena said while the cafes and restaurants looked welcoming and peaceful like in any other city, don't be fooled. She said that after dark, the city grows dangerous. "The gangs prefer to do their business at night, " said Elena. "The good people know to lock their doors and keep their kids in, if they can."

Max was aware of the violence in this country, as well as in other countries such as Honduras or Guatemala, where he had helped immigrants. He was not prepared for the level of violence, however, that his colleague revealed to him.

Elena said that while extortion was still the major economy, drugs had further jeopardized her people. "The major gangs are getting involved in the drug business, including prescription opiates, and they are fighting over drug turf." Elena blamed the United States for shipping its most violent criminals to El Salvador. "Some of these young people spent their whole life in the U.S. – having been taken there illegally as infants by their parents." She continued, "They are no more El Salvadoran than you are, Max. They are the ones who have implemented the strict gang culture code in my country. They recruit youths as young as ten to their 'new' families."

As Max listened, his shirt stuck to his neck in the humid air, and he heard the wails of a police car and an ambulance. Atop the police car sat a turret with a machine gun. The officer behind the gun, as well as the three other officers, had their faces covered with bandannas. "Don't expect them to stop," said Elena. "They are as afraid of the gangs as everyone else is."

Their discussion moved to Maria's legal plight as Max hoped that his colleague did not notice his sweaty shirt. Attorney Sanchez said that they had two problems. For one, Maria was insisting that Alisa and Roberto return to the United States immediately. Of course, they could leave tomorrow as U.S. citizens, but they refused to leave her. "I see," said Max. "I'm meeting with her tomorrow, if you can make it." "Of course," she said. "Number two," said Attorney Sanchez, "is that given the dangers in El Salvador, Maria's case is not that distinguishable from any other case. All these hundreds of folks in court seeking immigrant visas have cases as compelling as Maria's."

Max interrupted her. "You have to admit that the way Maria was tricked into leaving the U.S. would have influence on the immigration judge." "Yes," said Attorney Sanchez, "but affidavits have limited value. If Dr. Ryan admitted that he was behind this scheme and testified to that, I'm sure Maria would be given a visa." Max sighed. "I know we have no ability to force him to come to El Salvador." Elena said that the affidavits would be helpful, but they need live testimony by someone in El Salvador who can confirm what happened to Maria.

Later that night, Max settled into his small room at the Coronado Hotel. He telephoned Chelsea. She and Helene were scheduled to arrive in El Salvador the next day for the hearing. Max shared the legal challenges Maria faced. Chelsea told him that she had the names of the private investigators in the United States who tricked Maria. Max reiterated that unless they agree to testify before the immigration judge, their input would have limited value. "Even if I could get them to sign an affidavit, which is unlikely, the court will consider it like hearsay."

Max shared with Chelsea that he and Attorney Sanchez were going to see Maria and the children the next day. "I don't think Maria is ready to see you just yet, Chelsea," said Max. "She appreciates your coming here to testify," commented

 Max to a disappointed Chelsea. He explained that the family was in turmoil, as Maria was very worried about the children's safety.

Chelsea was about to hang up the phone when the name Oscar Cruz came into her mind. "I have it!" said an excited Chelsea. "I know who can give actual testimony as to what happened to Maria." In his guilt, her dad had given her more specifics about the deportation. "Oscar Cruz was their conduit in El Salvador. He was the one who rented the apartment to Maria and opened the bank account that my father funded." Chelsea then proceeded to give Max Oscar's phone number.

An intrigued Max greeted Attorney Sanchez at 9 a.m. the next morning. She had insisted on picking Max up, and in fact had even discouraged him from renting a car. "Don't draw any attention to yourself," Elena warned. Max had to admire Elena in her cream-colored pantsuit, which accentuated her exquisite skin. Seeking to impress Elena, Max had gone clothes hunting in the hotel store the previous night. His Dockers and simple collared shirt were replaced by a tropical suit that was similar in color to Elena's. "Well, don't you look like a local now," said a smiling Elena as Max entered her vehicle.

Max asked Elena if she had ever heard of a man named Oscar Cruz. "Yes," she said, "I have done some legal work for him." She explained that he owned numerous apartments in San Salvador, and she had helped him with the sale of one of his properties. Elena described Oscar as a popular Bon Vivant character who dressed well and went to the best restaurants in San Salvador. "He loves the ladies," laughed Elena, "but his charms did not work on me."

Max and Elena headed to Oscar's real estate office. Oscar's secretary laughed as Max asked if he could talk to Oscar. "He doesn't ever get up before noon. Leave me your number. Hopefully he will call you." Elena winked in Max's direction as she spoke to the secretary, "Tell Oscar that Elena Sanchez wants to speak to him."

Max and Elena's next stop was Maria's apartment. As they knocked on Maria's door, loud voices carried from within. A distraught Maria, hair disheveled and tissues in hand, opened the door. Although Max and Maria had talked extensively, they had never met. "I'm sorry," said Maria. "Please come in." Max introduced himself and Elena as Maria introduced her children, Alisa and Roberto.

Maria explained that the family was having a disagreement. Maria wanted her children to leave for the United States "today" as it was "unsafe" for them. "You go to Boston. I don't care what happens to me." Roberto adamantly proclaimed, "We are not leaving you here!" Alisa hugged her mother and whispered, "We love you." Turning to Max, Alisa asked, "They will give my mother a visa this week, right?" Attorney Sanchez responded in Spanish, " We will do everything we can to get the visa for your mom." A worried Roberto interjected, "What are the chances?" Max fudged a bit to relax them. "Very good," he said, while silently praying that he could get Oscar to testify in two days.

Max and Elena then prepared the family for the hearing. The two attorneys went over the family's testimony and even suggested what they should wear for the trial. As Max and Elena were leaving, Maria asked if she could talk to them outside. An exhausted Maria explained that she was worried because she had not paid her extortion fee in a month. She was terrified that the gangs might kidnap her children. Max reached into the pocket of his new suit and pulled out $400 in crisp hundred-dollar bills. As he handed them to Maria he told her, "This should satisfy them. Keep the kids in the house until the trial." An impressed Elena thought to herself, "Hmmm, he's not the most handsome man, but he's got a good heart."

Upon getting back to the Coronado Hotel, Max received a message from the clerk. Oscar Cruz would meet them in the hotel lounge at 7 p.m. The message said to make sure Attorney Sanchez was there. A smiling Elena said, "I wouldn't miss it."

Elena and Max were sipping margaritas in the lounge at 7 p.m. Max had to admit that Elena looked gorgeous tonight. Admiring guests were probably wondering what a woman like her was doing with him, thought Max. At 7:30, a loud voice yelled Elena's name and greeted her, "Hola, Senora Sanchez." Oscar then kissed her on both cheeks. Turning to Max, Oscar greeted the attorney like they were old friends. Max thought to himself, "I know why this guy is so successful. He is a real smooth operator." For all Oscar's gregarious personality, Max was not impressed with this man physically. In fact, he reminded Max a bit of himself. Oscar was short and slightly overweight, with a gray goatee. But his manicured nails and tailored clothing spoke to the fact that he cared about the impression he made.

After some small talk, mostly Oscar asking about Elena's personal life, Max brought up the trial. He told Oscar all of the unfortunate things that had happened to the Gomez family since the deportation. Max let Oscar know what his actions had caused before asking him for help.

Oscar said that part of his success as a businessman involved doing "favors" for his many friends. He admitted that many of those friends live in the United States, where he frequently traveled. He conceded that one of those friends was private detective Ed Corcoran from Boston. Oscar was careful not to admit to any liability, but acknowledged that he did know a "little" about the Gomez family. He believed they were involved with some rich doctor from Boston.

Max then got right to the point. "Look, we know you were the contact person when the family was deported. We have records that you opened a bank account for the family, and you own the apartment where they currently live. My problem is that I need someone to testify before the judge in the immigration hearing this week. The family is at severe risk of violence if they do not get out of here." Seemingly unmoved, Oscar called out for "tequila, straight" as he responded, "Isn't everyone at risk around here?"

Oscar's ebullient personality grew somber as he downed his drink. "Look," he said, "I'm successful here because I'm careful not to make enemies." He continued, "I'm even friendly with the gangs around here. I'm good to them, if you know what I mean, and they leave me alone. I'm out every night and never have any trouble. If I testify, I might make an enemy out of someone, and why would I want to do that?" Elena spoke out. "Oscar, all I can say is that these people used your friendship to hurt some good people, the Gomez family. One family member,

living in your apartment building, might not live long if she doesn't get a visa." As Oscar got up from the table, he smiled, and the attorneys heard his words as he left: "I'll think about it."

Two days later, Chelsea and Helene squeezed into the tight, humid hall of the immigration court. Dozens of families lined the hall, overflowing the limited seats. Babies cried as nervous tension radiated through the corridors. They were soon met by Maria, her children, and the two attorneys. Chelsea and Helene hugged a grateful Maria and her family. Attorney Sanchez explained in Spanish to Maria what would happen today. Elena was happy to see that the case was assigned to Judge Lydia Oliva. Her reputation was tough, but fair, and she was not afraid to dig deeply into a case, unlike some judges.

Soon a court officer told the Gomez parties to go to Courtroom C. Max looked around, but did not see Oscar Cruz. Both counsels thought that the one-hour hearing before Judge Oliva went as well as could be expected. Maria testified that officials came to her Boston home and threatened that her children would be adopted if the family did not leave immediately. Chelsea and her mom testified that these officials were phony, and Dr. Ryan had admitted to this fraudulent scheme. Judge Oliva agreed with Attorney Roosevelt, that if not for the ruse, Maria would probably still be in Boston today. What Judge Oliva did not agree with was that Maria's dangers were any greater than hundreds of families in the court today. The judge, in deep thought, added rather ominously, "You realize your evidence is all hearsay, Counselors. Is there no one to attest to this scheme?"

It was at this foreboding, delicate point of the trial that the courtroom door opened with a bang. In a resplendent white suit, Oscar Cruz made a grand entrance. Not very impressed by his entrance, Judge Oliva said, "Who do we have here?" "Sorry, your honor, but I just heard about this case. I am Maria Gomez's landlord." Foregoing legal decorum, the judge asked Oscar what he had to say.

In his flamboyant style, Oscar proceeded to own the courtroom in a way that would make Clarence Darrow jealous. Oscar confirmed that his American friends had concocted a scheme to deport the Gomez family. While he did not know why it had occurred, Oscar confirmed his role in securing an apartment and setting up the bank account for the family. He added, "While I have safe apartments, I am aware that this family is at real risk of violence." At the conclusion of his testimony, he was dismissed by the judge, and he strode out of the courtroom, mouthing to Elena, "Call me."

In Spanish, Judge Oliva then called Maria over to her bench. "Mrs. Gomez, I'm sorry about the loss of your husband. I believe you were deported here on false pretenses. Therefore, I am going to give you a visa." The courtroom erupted in emotion with the news. Max even kissed his co-counsel. Chelsea, Helene, and Maria fell into each other's arms with emotions of relief and happiness.

# Chapter 15: Maria's Return

CHELSEA AND HER MOM anxiously waited at the airport for Maria's flight from El Salvador to arrive. They had secured Maria and her children a rental apartment in Boston near their own. The three-bedroom apartment was owned by a colleague of Dr. Ryan's. Although she saw her dad infrequently, Chelsea was thankful that her dad had helped them get the apartment. Mrs. Ryan was going to pay the reasonable rent until Maria got on her feet.

Chelsea was not sure how Maria would react to her. Although they had briefly reunited at the hearing in San Salvador, Maria had not really talked to her in three years, and so much had happened to both families. Maria's former life in America had been turned upside down. Her husband had died, and her brother was in prison.

As the passengers came through the airport gates, Chelsea immediately recognized Alisa. A beautiful teenager with those dark curls and almond-shaped eyes, Alisa ran into Chelsea's arms. But Chelsea would have walked by Maria if it weren't for Alisa's recognition. Not able to be as observant in El Salvador, Chelsea now saw that Maria was thin, almost frail, with heaps of gray hair. With one arm around Alisa, Chelsea wrapped the other around Maria. All three women sobbed as the hugs got tighter and tighter. Helene hugged Roberto, who was now a tall, handsome young man. The emotion of the moment seemed to confuse him, as he stoically looked down at his feet.

Finally, Maria whispered, "Thank you, Chelsea." Despite the pain that surrounded all of them, Chelsea was happy to hear those words.

The ride to the family's apartment was both emotional and awkward. Small talk filled the car; "How was your flight," etc. to prevent the silence from being uncomfortable. Finally, arriving at the apartment, the family entered and looked around. Alisa ran from room to room, joyfully admiring her new home. "I have my own bedroom." Helene had used her talents to make the apartment comfortable. She had purchased simple furniture — bedroom sets, a kitchen table and chairs, and a sofa and television. The refrigerator was stocked with healthy foods. Even Roberto smiled as he checked out all the cable options on the television.

After the families had enjoyed some take-out pizza, Chelsea and Helene realized that Maria was tired and needed to unpack. They promised to come back the following day. They also gave the family a phone so that they would not feel alone.

As promised, Chelsea and her mom returned to the apartment the next day. Maria's family huddled around the television and declined the suggestion to check out the neighborhood. Maria's only request was to ask if she could speak with her brother Ramon.

In the next few days, which turned into weeks, Maria's family did not leave the apartment other than to purchase necessary food and toiletries. They were subdued and constantly looked out the windows. Maria did have an emotional telephone conversation with Ramon, but he encouraged her not to visit him in prison.

Eventually, the family shared with Chelsea and Helene bits and pieces of the last three years of their life in El Salvador. While Maria's Spanish was a bit more layered with Hispanic terms, she was understood. Her children, who spoke perfect English, filled in the details of her story.

Maria recalled that in those first few days, San Salvador reminded her of any city. Streets were bustling with shoppers; busses and autos sputtered through the clogged streets; and ambulance sirens were heard throughout the day. If not for the stifling heat that clung to her skin, Maria thought she could be in Boston. Maria said, "I tried to make things like normal for my family. I fixed up the apartment to make it a home. But Carlos was not himself. He seemed to sense danger."

Maria's opinion that this city was like Boston quickly changed, however. Here the nights were eerily quiet. People simply did not go out at night. The family quickly learned this when they ventured out at 6 p.m. one night to get an ice cream. Not only was the bustling-by-day store closed, but the family was confronted by a group of five teenagers.

"All I could remember that night was the Virgin of Guadalupe tattoo," stated Maria. The teenagers, none looked older than eighteen, surrounded the family. Its leader, a shirtless young man with the massive religious tattoo covering his chest, spoke, "What are you doing here?" The stunned family could not answer at first, given the sight before them.

Each of the bold youths were adorned in black or blue ink. Eyes, scalps, ears, and necks were covered by images and script. One had to look hard at their bodies to find clean flesh. "I'll never forget the daggers," offered Roberto. "Each of the group had what looked like the blade of a dagger stretching from below his eye to his mouth." The daggers accentuated the family's fears.

Again, the apparent leader said in a menacing voice, "What are you doing here?" Alisa responded, "We are just taking a walk." Carlos gathered his family close to him and tried to leave. He heard the words, "Where are you going, old man? You don't do anything around here without my permission." Trying to soften the tone, Maria said softly, "She is my savior." The leader, Eduardo, snapped, "What?" "The Virgin of Guadalupe; she is who I pray to." For once, the menacing look faded from Eduardo's face. "You like?" he asked. "Yes," said Maria, "She is very beautiful." Eduardo then turned to his gang. "You see, these Americanos aren't stupid." In response, the other gang members began to probe their own bodies, to identify their own religious images. This was difficult, as religious icons were interlaced with tattoos of barbed wire, guns, and spider webs. They hooted as they identified such religious images as Jesus Christ, the Holy Trinity, and praying hands on their bodies. "See mine!" yelled one in glee.

Roberto responded to Eduardo, "You know we are from America?" Eduardo smiled knowingly. "We know where you live, and how long you have been here. We also know you have money coming in from America. Now, you owe us rent." Carlos interrupted, "Rent for what?" "For living and walking on my street. You see, we own these streets, and you owe me fifty dollars. Every week, I will come to your apartment for my rent."

Recognizing the urgency of the situation, Maria hurriedly gave Eduardo fifty dollars. "Now go home," Eduardo ordered. "We don't want you here at night." The mystified family quickly went back to their apartment in silence. They felt lucky to be able to lock their door. Carlos looked at his family and promised, "I will get us out of here."

The next day, Maria heard a tap on the door. Resplendent in a white sombrero and matching suit was the smiling face of Oscar Cruz. He strode into her apartment like he owned it, which in fact he did. The family had met him briefly the night they were picked up at the airport by one of his assistants. Alisa instantly disliked this short, gregarious man, who stared at her a bit too long.

"You are a very lucky lady," said Oscar Cruz to Maria. "The authorities in America have paid for this apartment until you get your immigration case resolved. They are also going to put $300 each month into an account for you until you get settled here." Oscar then gave the family paperwork to access the account at the nearby Bank of El Salvador. Maria tried to question the origin of the account but was quickly admonished. Shaking his head vigorously, Oscar put his hands to his lips. "Don't ask any questions. That is very dangerous," he told Maria.

To the family's surprise, Oscar knew about their encounter with Eduardo the night before. "Just pay the money – they get rent just like me," he advised Maria. "You have to understand, these streets are owned by the gangs." Oscar then opened the blinds of the apartment. Looking out the window to the next block, Oscar warned the family, "Do not go to that side of the street. That is owned by another gang. If you go, you may be killed or raped," he said, now staring at Alisa.

"But how do my kids go to school?" asked a stunned Maria. "Ask your neighbors. Everyone knows how things work around here," directed Oscar. Now Maria understood why people in San Salvador seemed to zig-zag through the streets. They were forced to navigate away from enemy turf.

Putting his sombrero on his head and stopping to admire his image in the mirror, the brusque Oscar started to leave. "Wait, are you saying that Eduardo's gang owns us?" asked Roberto. A laughing Oscar nodded. "Yes, in a way. They will cut you up into small pieces and leave you in the street if you challenge them." Maria asked, "What about the police?" "What about them?" laughed Oscar.

"Well, don't they protect us?" Oscar replied, "We have two types of police. Some are as scared of the gangs as you. Why do you think they cover their faces on the street? The gangs will not only kill them, but kill their children." Maria and Carlos looked horrified.

"Yes, that has happened. The second group are the police who are members of the gang." In disbelief, Alisa asked, "The police work for the gangs?" "No senorita, they are members of the gang. So are many politicians, business owners, and even school teachers." Then adjusting his sombrero, a whistling Oscar walked out of the apartment to collect his other rents. The appalled family just watched in silence as Oscar called out, "Have a good day."

The following day, a nervous Maria and Carlos ventured out into the humid air to find work. Each cautioned Alisa and Roberto not to leave the apartment. "School will have to wait." Alisa laughed sarcastically to herself, "And I thought failing math was my biggest school concern in Boston." Roberto gladly played video games all day.

Maria came across a small café on her block with a tattered red sign that said "Nina's". A handsome woman about Maria's age greeted her in Spanish: "Hola. Me llamo es Nina." Maria smiled back. "Estas contratando?' (Are you hiring?) "Business is tough around here. I have to close early because it's too dangerous." Nina asked Maria if she was new to the neighborhood. After hearing about Maria's family situation, a sympathetic Nina said, "I couldn't pay you much. Can you cook pupusas?" Maria smiled. "I think you will be pleased with my pupusas." Then she talked about her job in Boston. Nina agreed to hire Maria, and asked her to start the next morning. Maria was happy, as much for the closeness of the job as for the $5.00 an hour salary.

...........................................................................

After listening to Maria's story, a privileged Chelsea realized that she had to learn why El Salvador was so violent. Over the next few months, she learned more about that country's history.

Years of civil war in the 1980s, and a lack of political leadership had created a vacuum that normalized violence by 2008. The United States had contributed to El Salvador's instability by pouring billions into the military led by the right-wing government. Massive deportations of gang members from the U.S. brought an Americanized gang structure to the poor country. In addition to carjacking, robbery, and murder, the whole country operated on an extortion system that had the powerful preying on the powerless. In fact, extortion was the economic base of the country. Chelsea read that by 2008, El Salvador, a country of 6.5 million people, had an estimated 500,000 gang members. It was also called the murder capital of the world, with one murder occurring every two hours.

One night a week later, Chelsea went by Maria's apartment with some new bedding that she had purchased. Maria was cooking pupusas in the kitchen. Chelsea had been thinking about Maria and her family, and why the subject of Carlos's death never arose. Chelsea hesitantly asked about Carlos.

Perhaps it was the memory of her times with her "bicha," cooking in the Ryans' kitchen, that made Maria open up to Chelsea about the murder of Carlos.

# Chapter 16: Murder in San Salvador

Over pupusas, Maria revealed how her beloved husband Carlos had died. Maria said she was working at Nina's for about a week when a familiar face walked in. The young gang leader with the Virgin of Guadalupe tattoo appeared. He proceeded to give Nina a kiss. Nina introduced Maria to her son, Eduardo. The young man smiled at Maria and said, "We've met." Maria had trouble looking at him as she continued to wipe down one of the tables. "Ola," she whispered. "Ola to you," said Eduardo. "She loves my tattoo, Mom," said Eduardo to his obviously proud mother. "Got to go back to work, Mom. See you later, Maria," he said as he winked at her. "Be careful, son," said Nina.

Over the next few days, Nina shared her personal history with Maria as the busy lunch period wound down. "Eduardo is my only child. His father used to beat me so often that Eduardo would not leave my bed. He knew, even at age three, that my nights were dangerous. His dad would come home drunk at night, and that was when he beat me. My Eduardo was so smart, Maria, that even at three he knew that his father would not beat me with his son in the bed." Maria asked how she got the beatings to stop. Nina laughed nonchalantly. "I stabbed the bastard." Maria did not ask if she killed Eduardo's dad.

As time went on, Nina started to view Maria more as a friend than as an employee. She shared her worries about Eduardo. "I know he is in the gang. He had no choice. He needed a man in his life, and the older members took him under their care." Maria asked how old he was when he joined the gang.

"Probably around age twelve. It's not all bad, Maria, but I worry."

It seemed Nina had somehow come to terms with Eduardo's profession. "I hate to say this, but boys have to join the gangs just to stay safe." Maria asked if the police would help her. Nina snickered, "The police? They are worse than the gangs. They kill more people than the gangs. That's why they wear the balaclavas. No one can see them when they commit crimes." Nina defended her son, who even as a child had protected her. "He is a good boy. He has a good heart, and he does not hurt anyone who does not deserve it."

A smiling Eduardo was a daily presence in the restaurant. One day he took Maria outside. "You did not tell my mom about our rent, right?" Maria shook her head negatively. "Good. My mother doesn't know what I do, and I want to keep it that way. Understand?" Maria nodded. After a long moment, Eduardo said, "I see your kids are not in school." A surprised Maria was about to ask how he knew, but Eduardo added, "I know everything that goes on around here. This is my neighborhood." Maria said, "I do not send them because they might go in the wrong neighborhood, and I am afraid for them." Eduardo told her, "Have them ready at 7:30 tomorrow morning. I will walk them to school."

The next day, a nervous Roberto and Alisa met Eduardo just outside their apartment. They had no idea where the school was or if the school knew of their existence. As they walked with Eduardo, they soon realized that he was a very popular young man in their neighborhood. Motorists rolled down their windows and waved at him. Alisa asked, "Do you know all these people?" Eduardo smiled and answered, "They are asking my permission to ride in the neighborhood." When others flashed their lights at him, Roberto asked, "More permission?" Eduardo laughed, "You're getting it."

Periodically on their short walk together, Eduardo would stop in various stores. He would come out counting money. An impressed Roberto asked, "Rent?" Eduardo just smiled. During their walks to school, Eduardo also counseled the students. "Don't walk there; be careful of that guy." In one neighborhood, Eduardo saw a rival gang member on the street corner. He raised his finger like a gun and shouted, "Tonight." This was the only time Eduardo was not smiling on their short trip.

Robert and Alisa were surprised when the school principal was expecting them. He placed the nearly eighteen-year-old Roberto in the intermediate school, and the sixteen-year-old Alisa in the middle school.

The youths soon learned that schools were far different in San Salvador than in Boston. Roberto found himself sharing old math books with three other students. Alisa read books that were for fourth graders.

While the teachers appeared to want to help students, several factors worked against them.

The classes were huge and the heat was oppressive. Alisa thought that the teachers seemed almost fearful of the students. One day, a savage fight occurred in her classroom. As the other children watched, the teacher remained in his seat. It stopped when the teacher told the smiling perpetrator that he was dismissed for the day. The teacher must have recognized the horror in Alisa's face. "This is how things work around here," he affirmed.

One day, Roberto was cornered by a group of students. "You owe us money, Americano," demanded one of them. "You have to pay us ten dollars per week to go to school here. If you don't, we might take your sister."

That night, Alisa and Roberto told their parents about the encounter at school. Carlos exploded, "I will kill them." He grabbed his jacket and ran out of the apartment. This episode highlighted a recent familiar and troubling pattern for Carlos. Unable to find work in San Salvador, the normally quiet Carlos had grown increasingly angry in the home. Even Maria, whom he adored, could not get Carlos out of this temperament.

The nights when Carlos went out continued to increase. He would come home several hours later intoxicated, and barely able to walk.

These actions from a man who used to drink rum only once a year at Christmas. The mornings after, Carlos would awake embarrassed. He would apologize to his family and vow never to do it again. But his behavior only worsened in the ensuing weeks.

One night, Eduardo came to the Gomez apartment to collect his rent. "Since you work for my mother, I will take ten dollars less," he said to Maria with his familiar smile. His mood darkened, however, and he asked to speak to Carlos. As Carlos was out again, Eduardo addressed the rest of the family. He warned that Carlos's behavior was an embarrassment to the community, and the family must keep Carlos home at night. "I can only protect him so much. My bosses tell me how to run things."

Maria had quickly absorbed how tightly the gangs controlled the neighborhoods. People were often told to be off the streets by 7 p.m. This allowed the gangs to work their crime operations with fewer witnesses. House parties were silenced on weekends if the gangs found them too loud. Carlos was not the first person to be cautioned for public intoxication. The murderous gangs had an ironic code of honor.

On one night, when Carlos returned from his nightly sojourn, his bad behavior escalated. He slapped Maria as she attempted to undress him. He screamed at Alisa, "This is all your fault!" His drunken berating of his family went on for hours, until he passed out.

Upon awakening, the family saw a small piece of paper on the kitchen table. Carlos apologized and said he would not be home until he got a job. But Carlos did not return that day, or the next. Frantic, Maria and the children roamed the neighborhood looking for him. Over Eduardo's objections, they even went into a rival gang's territory. On one such foray they saw the body of a middle-aged man in a vacant lot. It was not unusual in San Salvador to find unclaimed bodies lying in the street for days. On their way to school, children often walked by these decedents. Alisa had walked by such a victim for several days in a row. The lifeless youth, not more than fifteen, had his feet and hands cut off. Eduardo told her that a message had been sent by a rival gang. Remarkably, even Alisa and Roberto soon became immune to these terrible sights. To dispose of the bodies, masked government officials periodically made group "death" retrievals on the streets.

As the family entered the vacant lot, Maria forced herself to go up to the body of the man.

Fortunately, decomposition had not set in, and Maria made the sign of the cross on the corpse. It was not Carlos.

Two weeks after Carlos's disappearance, Maria was contacted by the police. She was told to come to the station to identify someone. The dead man was her beloved Carlos. Maria kissed the face of the kind husband who had saved her life crossing the Rio Grande. Roberto and Alisa hugged the man who was tormented to death in this perilous country.

Maria's tears were barely dried when the policeman told her to bury Carlos immediately and quietly. "Aren't you going to investigate his death?" Maria asked. The policeman responded patronizingly, "Lady, go home. Bury your husband. There is nothing to investigate." For once, Maria would not budge. "I want you to find out who killed my husband," she demanded. The policeman calmly stated, "It is dangerous for you to pursue this." With that, the officer pulled down his lower lip to show her his telltale tattoo. Maria realized the policeman was an active member of the gang. Alisa and Roberto dragged their mother out of the police station. They buried Carlos privately the next day, in a nearby cemetery.

Over the following months, Roberto grew troubled by the pressure at school. The gang member who initially asked him for rent wanted Roberto to join his gang. "We will take care of you, Roberto. No one will disrespect you again if you join us." Roberto had to admit that the gang life held interest for him. School was boring, and he was tired of not being able to help his family. He also saw the respect that gang members like Eduardo had in the community.

Still, Roberto knew that his mother could absorb only so much loss. As he weighed his options, the gang's threats grew more ominous. One day, as Roberto and Alisa walked home from school, a car blocked their path. The car door opened, and several of the youths Roberto recognized from school threw him to the ground. Then they forced Alisa into their car and sped away.

Frantic, Roberto ran to Nina's restaurant where his mom was working. "They took Alisa," shouted Roberto. Maria's screams alerted Nina in the kitchen. "Go home," said Nina after learning what had happened. "I will call Eduardo." Knowing no one else to turn to, mother and son went back to their apartment and cried and prayed for Alisa. Within an hour, a tearful Alisa burst through the door, accompanied by Eduardo. Too traumatized to even talk, a sobbing Alisa collapsed in her mother's arms. Maria asked over and over if the boys hurt her. She shook her head no, over and over. Eduardo said, "She will be okay. They did not have time to touch her. Don't worry. We will get our revenge. They have sisters, too."

Sickened at the violence around her, Maria led her daughter into the bedroom. "Come, mi amor. I will take care of you."

Alone with Roberto, Eduardo said, "You must join us now. Your sister and your mother are not safe. These men would have raped Alisa, and could have killed her. Your family's only hope is if you are one of us."

After putting Alisa to bed, Maria returned to the living room where Roberto and Eduardo were talking. Roberto was resolved. "Mama, I am going with Eduardo. This is the only way."

Maria begged him not to. "We will move to the country, away from San Salvador." Roberto scoffed, "The gangs are just as bad in the country – even worse. At least this way I can protect my family," said Roberto as he started to follow Eduardo out the door. Maria grabbed Roberto by his waist and blocked his way. "Please, Mama, let me go." "No!" shouted Maria hysterically. "I can't take another death in my family! Please, Roberto. I want you and

Alisa to go back to America. You cannot stay here. I will be fine." Maria fell to her knees, holding onto Roberto's ankles. "No, Mama, this is the only way," said Roberto as he gently removed her tight grip and walked out the door to meet Eduardo.

Alisa had been listening and came down to join her mother. They wrapped their arms around each other and crumpled to the floor. "I'm so sorry, Mama." Maria could only repeat, "Thank you, God, for saving my daughter." As Maria's thoughts turned to her son, she felt a despair like none she had ever experienced. For the only time in her life, she wished she was dead. She got on her knees and asked God for forgiveness and mercy. She asked for an angel to save her family. He arrived within twenty-four hours: a disheveled angel named Max.

# Chapter 17: Roberto's Test

HAVING PUSHED HIS MOTHER AWAY, Roberto followed Eduardo into the quiet streets of San Salvador. Eduardo stopped and turned to Roberto, "Go home to your mother. I will call you tomorrow, Roberto. You can meet my boss then." Roberto obeyed and returned to his home. He walked right into his room and shut the door. A grateful Maria and Alisa watched wordlessly, careful not to upset him any further.

The next day, Saturday, a nervous Roberto awoke with the dawn. He carefully dressed. He put two layers of shirts on top of long underwear. He was not sure what to expect today, but he had heard the gang initiation could be brutal. Massive assaults by the group's members could go on and on. They wanted to gauge their potential member's toughness.

Eduardo called later that morning. "Meet me at my mother's restaurant at noon. We will meet the boss this afternoon." Again, scarcely a word was spoken in the quiet home. As Roberto got ready to leave, Maria tightened her grip on her rosary beads, which were often found in her hands these days. "Be careful," she whispered to her son as he walked out the door.

Eduardo and Roberto were soon driving along the bustling streets of San Salvador. Saturday was the busiest day of the week, with many of the citizens off from work venturing out to shop. Even the gangs seemed to loosen their tight grip on the community on this day. People could walk across blocks of enemy turf to get to their destination more quickly.

Roberto listened as Eduardo talked on and on about his boss. The man's name was Mario Ramirez. Eduardo appeared to idolize this man. "He wants to change everything around here," he told Roberto. "He thinks we play right into the government's hands by killing each other. He's right – the police and the government are our enemies. You will see, Roberto. He is a very smart man."

Roberto soon found himself in San Salvador's historic center. Since it was a Saturday, thousands of street vendors set up their rickety carts and hawked their wares. Country farmers sold their vegetables; craftsmen sold hand-made jewelry, and others hawked electronics and CDs.

Roberto had been to the market once before. His mother had taken him and his sister on Saturday when they had first arrived, two years ago. He smiled when he remembered his mother biting into a pupusa at one stall. "Too dry," she whispered to Roberto as she praised the elderly merchant's food.

Roberto recalled how impressed he was when he first viewed this lively center. It reminded him of Boston's Faneuil Hall. It consisted of a series of small squares surrounded by monuments of El Salvador's past military leaders and politicians. The main square was framed by two impressive buildings: the National Palace, and the Cathedral, where the slain Archbishop Romero once said Mass before thousands of El Salvadoran worshippers.

Like everything in the chaotic country, thought Roberto at the time, he would have probably been more impressed with the center one hundred years ago. Decades of molten bird stains tarnished buildings amidst crumbling mortar. Merchants gathered at the foot of weathered monuments, their tarpaulins sprawled against the figures of past presidents.

But today, Roberto was more focused on the sights and sounds of thousands of San Salvadorans shopping. Eduardo said, "All these merchants pay us one dollar a day to sell here." "All of them?" asked Roberto, assessing the thousands of merchants in the area. "Not yet," said a smiling Eduardo. "But we are slowly getting control of all of them." Roberto was surprised to be led to the second floor of a smart building overlooking the main square. He was soon face to face with one Mario Ramirez.

Ramirez was not the type of man Roberto expected. His face and body were free of tattoos. His handsome face was surrounded by black styled hair and a paper-thin mustache. He wore a blue polo shirt and neatly pressed brown khakis. To Roberto, Ramirez seemed like a preppy college student.

"How is your sister?" Ramirez asked Roberto without any introduction. Before Roberto could answer, the man added, "The government treats us like animals, and that's what we have become." Eduardo, sitting at the back of the room, agreed, "Right boss."

With a nod toward Eduardo, Ramirez put out his hand to Roberto. "I'm Mario Ramirez. Eduardo has told me a lot about you."

Roberto was so stunned, he was barely able to respond, "I'm Roberto." To Roberto, this classy man who spoke perfect English was nothing like any other gang member he had seen. Examining Roberto's face, Ramirez commented, "I know what you are thinking. You didn't expect to meet someone like me today. But I didn't expect to be in San Salvador either. I lived in California my whole life, brought to the U.S. when I was two. I was at the top of my class in high school. I was going to attend college, probably USC or UCLA. Unfortunately, I got caught selling marijuana, and they sent me here. Crazy, huh? I heard you got deported too?" Roberto, rather surprised at this conversation, replied, "Some rich family got us deported from Boston."

"Figures," Ramirez said with a sarcastic laugh. "Get the brown guys. I ran my marijuana business with all these preppy white kids in California. Their parents got them off with fancy attorneys. I was the only one who got in trouble. They sent my ass here before I knew it. Fuck America! They rely on us to do the jobs no one else wants, and then dispose of us when we are of no more use." Roberto connected with Ramirez. "America was not a fair country," he agreed.

Ramirez quizzed Roberto. "How about you, Roberto? What are your plans? College?" "Not really," said Roberto. "I like to work with my hands. I want to get a trade and make sure my mother doesn't have to work again."

"Good," said Ramirez, although he sounded disappointed. "That's honorable. Something we need more of around here." Looking out the window at the market, Ramirez said out loud, "I want to create a new economy in this country. See all those people in the stalls? Half of them pay me rent to sell here. The other half pay rent to a man right across the street from us." Ramirez pointed to a similar building on the other side of the square. "This man's name is Hector. But he is not like me, Roberto. He is stupid. I tell him, let's work together. Instead of fighting each other, we should fight the politicians in fancy suits. We should fight the police who hide their faces, but have death squads that kill us in the middle of the night."

Roberto continued, "I tell Hector, you know the Federales put enemy gang members in the same cells to kill each other. That's what they want – for us to kill each other. But he's okay with that. So I have to eliminate him to achieve my dreams for El Salvador."

"What about the government?" asked Roberto. "Don't they want peace for the people?" "The government," scoffed Ramirez. "Let me tell you about them. About three years ago, a new president came in. He had a new approach. No more 'con mano dura' or the 'Iron Fist' approach for the people. The government actually paid us not to take rent from all these peasants." Ramirez looked down at the thousands of vendors as he spoke. "The government got us jobs and improved the jails. And it worked, Roberto. Even stupid Hector could see the changes. We didn't have to kill each other."

"So what happened?" asked Roberto. Ramirez slowly shook his head as he answered, "What happened is a new president came in and the Iron Fist returned. The people? The government doesn't care about the people. It's the people in power who love the chaos. That's how they stay rich. But I have a better plan for the people of El Salvador."

"You see, Roberto, even if Hector and I collect a dollar a day from all these peasants, there is only so much money changing hands. We have to grow the economy, Roberto, and that's what I want to do. I want Eduardo to be wearing a business suit one day, overseeing all his real estate holdings." "I agree, boss," said a smiling Eduardo.

"You might be very valuable for my business model Roberto. You have dual citizenship, and Boston is a large market for my business. "What business?" asked Roberto. "Drugs," said Ramirez, "Not drugs like marijuana or cocaine. No, legal drugs. The type that Americans take for all their pain and anxieties. I'm talking prescription medications like oxycodone and Zanax."

"You see, we are already working with the Mexicans and the Columbians in this drug business. I now have labs in El Salvador that make ecstasy and crystal meth. Those other countries' labs were shut down as a result of international police efforts. This leaves our country free to make as much as we want to," smiled Ramirez.

"I have seen the future, Roberto," said the ambitious Ramirez. "And it is with the pills." He held up what looked like a 25-ounce coffee travel mug and said, "Five million." Roberto was amazed, "Five million dollars?" "Yes, we can soon produce a new drug in our labs called fentanyl. It is 50 to 100 times stronger than heroin. It can be shipped to America in a container this size. Then they mix their oxys with this fentanyl. You see, Roberto, I want to be the Bill Gates of El Salvador. What do you think?"

"What do you want me to do?" asked a hesitant Roberto.

"Well, obviously we need people to distribute the pills once they get to Boston. That would be your job—to organize their distribution. Get some good people that you trust to get the pills into schools and businesses."

Roberto thought it sounded dangerous, and told Ramirez so.

"For who? For the people who screwed your family and deported you? They don't care about you, and if we don't do it, someone else will get in the game. These pills aren't going away in America. The Americans need these pills to get through the day. All the Americans should be shipped to El Salvador to see what real stress is like," Ramirez laughed sarcastically.

Roberto said, "I mean it might be dangerous for me." Ramirez reassured him, "First, the worst they can do is deport you back to this shithole. I will have a team of lawyers to help you if you are arrested. Trust me." Roberto heard a laugh from the back of the room, followed by, "I like it, boss."

Ramirez suddenly stood up, a sign that told Roberto the meeting was over. "You think about what I said, Roberto. I think we can make a lot of money together. Now, go with Eduardo. I think he has a surprise for you."

After the meeting, Eduardo encouraged Roberto to join with Ramirez. "I told you, Roberto, Mario is amazing. He is so smart. What do you think?" Careful not to disclose his true feelings, Roberto stated, "Sounds good to me."

On the way back to Roberto's home, Eduardo detoured to a dilapidated house in a poor residential neighborhood. The house looked vacant. Roberto knew the gangs often moved into such homes – often evicting the people living there. This way, the gangs were able to keep a close eye on the neighborhood.

Roberto was led to the basement of the home. All the windows had been darkened. A figure sat slumped in the middle of the room with his hands tied behind his back. Also present were some of Eduardo's menacing friends who had approached the Gomez family that first night. The slumped man had already been beaten – blood dripped from his red-soaked shirt to the floor. Eduardo spoke:" I told you he would pay, Roberto." Then Roberto realized that before him sat the person from school who had first asked him for rent. "That's the one who kidnapped your sister, right?" shouted Eduardo to the forlorn figure. "You're sorry, right?" "Si, Roberto," answered the bloody youth.

Eduardo handed Roberto a knife. "You must avenge your sister's honor, Roberto. Cut him." A stunned Roberto was filled with both anger and sympathy. He picked up the knife and said to Alisa's abductor, "Were you going to rape my sister?" "No, please, we just wanted to scare her so you would join us," the boy pleaded. "Why the fuck would he go with you?" said Eduardo. "He's with us." A growing anger in Roberto overcame his sympathy. He was angry at this teenager.

But he was also angry that he had to live here, surrounded by this violence. He was angry that if he did not stab his classmate, he would be considered weak by the gang.

As Roberto fingered the knife, contemplating all these thoughts, a voice emerged in his head. It was that of his Uncle Ramon. In his frequent calls from prison, Ramon reminded Roberto that he was now the man of the house. Ramon's parting words were always the same: "Make your mother proud." Roberto wordlessly dropped the knife. "It's okay, Roberto, we will teach you. For now we will take care of him. Come, I'll take you home."

Roberto rode in silence with Eduardo as they drove home. He contemplated that maybe

Ramirez was right – no one cared about them. Maybe the drug business wasn't so bad.

He left Eduardo and walked into the family's apartment, still pondering his situation. His thoughts were interrupted by voices in the kitchen. They were the voices of Max Roosevelt and Elena Sanchez. His mother's smiling face greeted Roberto. "These attorneys are going to help us to get out of here." A dubious Roberto muttered to himself, "What bullshit."

Four days later, Maria got her visa and the family was flying back to Boston. Roberto never got to say goodbye to Eduardo. He would always wonder if Alisa's kidnapper had survived.

# Chapter 18: Dr. Ryan's Grief

IN THE WEEKS AND MONTHS following Maria's return to the United States, both families attempted to heal and move on. Chelsea continued to live with her mom and started taking courses at Boston University. Helene continued her therapy with Dr. Greene and prepared to attend law school in the fall.

After several weeks, the Gomez family tentatively ventured out of the safety of their apartment. Maria joined a therapy group of fellow Central American women touched by violence. She also volunteered at a local immigration shelter. Maria slowly regained her love of cooking by feeding the shelter's grateful families, who received her pupusas. She talked to her brother Ramon several times by phone. He still resisted Maria's desire to see him, however.

Alisa, a radiant young woman of sixteen, entered the sophomore class of Boston High School. On the surface she was bubbly and outgoing, and popular with her classmates. She often brought them home to eat her mother's treats. Chelsea and her mother tried without success to convince Alisa to go to therapy. She refused, saying, "I want to look forward." Her demons might have to wait until she is ready, thought Chelsea.

Roberto, now nineteen, enrolled in an apprentice plumber's program with help from Boston's vocational services. He had been out of school nearly three years at that point and wanted to acquire the means to support his family.

Helene and Chelsea consciously did not see Maria's family often. It was just easier on everyone. There was so much hurt intertwined between both families that a respectful distance seemed best.

Chelsea had so many questions for Alisa, but on the rare occasion that they were alone, Alisa's happy demeanor prevented Chelsea from daring to approach the painful subject of Jon.

Chelsea's relationship with her dad continued as tepid. She spoke to him occasionally, but everything was of a surface nature. On one phone call, she started talking about Maria, and Dr. Ryan politely ended the call. Chelsea had not confronted her dad about her meeting with the investigator, Ed Corcoran. Part of her was afraid that her dad would have liability for his actions. For now, she was preoccupied with Maria and her family.

Chelsea learned that her dad no longer performed surgery. His life consisted of teaching at various medical schools in Boston. He'd also linked up with a medical sales company which promoted a new, less invasive form of hip and knee surgery. Dr. Ryan used his considerable reputation and contacts to promote the surgical innovation at hospitals throughout the country. Consequently, he was frequently away from Boston. This work schedule added more distance to his relationship with Chelsea.

By the fall of 2009, it was closing in on the first year of Jon's murder. Chelsea and Helene planned an anniversary Mass at the church where Jon had been buried a year earlier. The Mass was scheduled for the first Monday after Thanksgiving.

Chelsea naturally notified her dad of the Mass. She was stunned when he said he would not be attending. His excuse was that he would be out of town, visiting the family of the woman he was now dating. Chelsea learned that this woman was a thirty-something nurse at the hospital he'd formerly led. Chelsea imagined it was probably one of the many nurses who had fawned over her dad at the hospital. Helene was also upset that he would miss Jon's Memorial Mass.

While this Thanksgiving had a special significance for the Gomez family, who were grateful to be in a free and safe country, it brought Chelsea and Helene sad memories of their loss of Jon. They remembered how he had been so excited during his first weeks at the college, meeting new classmates and teammates. His roommate, Michael, was also a pre-med student, and they had shared their anxiety over their demanding coursework. Michael was not an athlete, and he offered to take good notes for Jon whenever Jon had a game. In fact, his first test notes were waiting in Jon's dorm room the night he was murdered. Mother and daughter spent the sad day relaying similar stories about Jon.

On the day of the Memorial Mass, the church was filled to capacity with mourners praying for Jon. Friends, hospital personnel, high school and college classmates and teammates were in attendance. Some, who were forced to wait outside, strained to hear the prayers emanating from inside. Chelsea and her mom had chosen the music and religious prayers that were significant to Jon.

Sitting alone in the rear of the church with his head bowed was Dr. Ryan. Recognized by many, he quickly left the Mass after it was over. Chelsea was surprised and pleased when told he was seen at the Mass. His telephone went to voicemail, however, when she attempted to call him.

After he fled from the church, Dr. Ryan drove to a place that had quieted his mind over the years in times of crises. He sat back and began to think about his past.

Growing up, his best memories were of summer Sundays at Hull Beach, a coastal town twenty miles south of Boston. His iron-worker dad had only Sundays off, and every week all of the four children eagerly changed into bathing suits following Mass. His normally gruff dad even whistled occasionally as he loaded the car with beach chairs and umbrellas. His mom seemed relieved of her everyday burdens as she prepared snacks and sandwiches for the family. Following a long day in the sun, the now red-skinned Irish clan would walk over to the arcades and amusements which lined the beach. His dad would give him and his older brother John money to ride their favorite ride, the cyclone.

It was during college that Dr. Ryan found this peaceful area near Hull Beach. Due east, past the last remnants of arcades at Hull Beach, past the recently built condominiums, lay Parsons Beach—not really a beach, but a rocky peninsula that jutted out to almost kiss the Boston skyline. From here, Dr. Ryan could observe the strong currents lace upon nearby Spectical Island. He could watch the airplanes descend through the clouds to nearby Logan Airport. He could view the tall buildings that framed the Boston Skyline, many of which his father had helped build.

Dr. Ryan recalled that his dad said working high up in these buildings never frightened him. "Forty feet or four hundred feet; you're dead anyway." It was hard work for hard men, and his dad, often working six days a week, never complained. The family, who lived in the Brighton section of Boston, never had to worry about whether there was enough food in the kitchen or whether their simple house would be foreclosed. His mom was a no-nonsense, street smart woman who on bad days cynically realized that getting married out of high school was not the best decision. She never complained, however - a classic Irish stoic- and seemed happiest on her weekly foray to the local casino with her two sisters.

Looking out at the gray harbor, Dr. Ryan thought of his brother John. John was his hero, as outgoing and handsome as Dr. Ryan was thin and bookish. The one person who could put a smile on his dad's face, even after his hard day at work, was John. An outgoing prankster, John could mimic anyone's voice or mannerisms. Even his parents had to laugh when John impersonated his mom's sisters getting ready to go to the casino. Raspy-voiced, with a cigarette in his mouth, John would say, "Let's beat the bastards at the casino tonight." John was also fawned over by Dr. Ryan's younger sisters, Fiona and Sara. But they seemed to view him, their other brother, as a bookish geek; often teasing their parents by asking if they took home the right baby. Dr. Ryan's distant relationship with both his sisters today was a sign to him that they still had those feelings.

John was a tremendous football player. His dad, who Dr. Ryan never heard utter the word "love," came close by keeping newspaper articles of John's football exploits in his wallet. When he entered his senior year in high school, John was considered the best quarterback in the city. Colleges were interested in him until they looked at his grades. A self-described "knucklehead," John had since childhood detested school. Dr. Ryan recognized today that he probably had undiagnosed ADHD with nervous energy that made studying difficult. This nervous energy contributed to his success on the football field, as he had dodged and twirled for many rushing touchdowns. When John was not playing football, he was always out and about with friends, rarely sleeping. Dr. Ryan sighed ruefully as he thought that if John grew up in Wellesley, he would have received care for his disorder and gone to college on a scholarship.

John had a special relationship with his younger brother. John admired his brother's keen intellect. Unlike the neighborhood youths, who teased Jim returning from the library with a stack of books in his arms, John encouraged his reading. "I wish I could sit and read like you," John often told his brother. In one of his last conversations, Dr. Ryan remembered what John said to him: "Jim, you will make our family proud one day."

John was killed the summer he entered his senior year of high school. He was a passenger in a car driven by another teammate when an older driver coming from the opposite direction lost control after a heart attack and crashed into them. Both boys were seriously injured, but John's teammate survived. Dr. Ryan's decision to become a surgeon emanated from that event. For John did not die right away, despite massive internal injuries. Doctors worked feverishly for two days, performing multiple surgeries. As they fixed one organ, another organ failed. Through it all, Jim sat with his parents and sisters admiring the passion and compassion of the doctors. When the tearful doctor told his father they could do no more for John, it was the only time he saw his dad cry.

As Dr. Ryan sat admiring the ocean, marveling that the same water may have drifted out of England weeks ago, his mind returned to his son Jon. The naming of his son was no accident. He wanted his son to have the same qualities as his brother, without the self-described "knucklehead" mentality. And in Dr. Ryan's mind, his son had fulfilled that wish. Jon was a great athlete with a superior intellect.

As he sat at the beach, Jim asked himself questions he normally avoided. Was it possible that he'd merged his brother into his son so completely, he was blinded to Jon's faults? Was he guilty of a form of psychological projection from his brother to his son? Did this somehow tragically lead to Jon's death? He rebuked himself for thinking these thoughts now. His son was absolutely not capable of committing a molestation!

In this quiet scene, Dr. Ryan sat on the beach mourning his son. He could not escape the fact that his fingerprints had led to Jon's murder. He wished that he had never gone to Ed Corcoran for help. He wished now that he had gone to the authorities, since he knew his son was innocent. Dr. Ryan was not comforted by the help he'd provided to Maria in El Salvador. He regretted stopping the monthly payment to her when his son was murdered. As he sat there, he simply cried until his tear ducts were dry.

# Chapter 19: Ramon's Incarceration

RAMON GOMEZ, INMATE NUMBER 4190 at Chauncey Correctional Institute, arose in his cage. He had been at Chauncey for one year now. Before even splashing water on his face, he knelt down to pray. A small plastic Madonna, a gift from his sister Maria, sat mounted above his sink that was once ceramic white, but was now gray like everything around him. The only item not gray was his orange jumpsuit, courtesy of the state of Vermont.

Ramon had not started his incarceration on his knees. In fact, he arrived an angry and sullen inmate. His ire went beyond the violation of his niece. He viewed America as a land for the privileged. Dark people who spoke a foreign language were not welcome. Ramon also raged against the people on both sides of the conflict of his beloved El Salvador. Each day that he opened his eyes in his cell, Ramon considered what life would have been like on his farm in his homeland. That was all he had wanted out of life – to be a farmer like his own dad.

When Ramon arrived at the prison, he was a bit of a celebrity. He was one of only three inmates who had been convicted of murder. The other four hundred or so inmates were there on lesser charges. Many were repeat offenders who stole to quiet their drug addiction. Although Ramon initially preferred to eat alone in silent anger, he was immediately befriended by two inmates from Central America. One, Jose, was from Guatemala, and the other, Santiago, was from Honduras.

The three initially bonded over the similarities of their lives in Central America. All three friends had grown up in rural areas. Long days went by quicker as the men shared stories of their families. Ramon even shared with his friends the loss of his brother Luis – his best friend. Jose, a diminutive, gap-toothed extrovert of about thirty, loved his life in America. He had five children from three women, and laughed to his friends, "I'll have more when I get out." The more reserved Santiago, who was about the same age and height as Jose, was often teased by Jose. He called Santiago "loco" for this quiet man's tendency to laugh at a sad story and remain stoic during a funny story.

Ramon soon realized that his two friends ran a thriving drug business. Jose, the brains of the pair, had efficient connections outside and inside the prison. Guards looked the other way during recreation periods as Santiago delivered orders to his "client" inmates. The naïve Ramon became aware of this business one day as he watched the frenzied Santiago run from one group to another. Apparently, a person in one of these groups was unhappy with an "order" from Santiago. Ramon watched as Santiago was punched and kicked repeatedly by a tall inmate known as "Bear." Guards quickly took Bear and the unconscious Santiago to the "hole," or the seclusion cells.

Jose approached Ramon one day at lunch and made him an offer. With his sly smile, Jose said to Ramon, "I need a new partner, and since you are a convicted murderer, no one wants to mess with you." Ramon was angry at Jose. He did not consider himself a murderer. No, he had acted out of a sense of justice. He told Jose in no uncertain terms that their friendship was over. Ramon was not a drug dealer, and he would not violate his parents' memory by doing something so wrong. As Ramon walked away, Jose called out, "I'll pay you for protection."

Ramon returned to his introverted state in prison. The days passed in a mundane pattern: a breakfast of scrambled eggs at 7 a.m., ham and cheese or some other sandwich at 11:30, rice and some kind of meat at 3:30, and lights out at 9:00 p.m., until another day begins. Aside from a menial job Ramon had in the kitchen for three hours, each day resembled the next. In his solitude, Ramon rehearsed over and over in his mind all the events that had landed him in prison. He blamed his country for the violence which caused the family's departure to America. He blamed Dr. Ryan and government officials for the unfair deportation of Maria and her family. Ramon blamed everyone but himself for his troubles.

One day during recreation period in the prison yard, Ramon saw a familiar face approach him. All the inmates looked at Ramon as if they expected an altercation. The thick, heavily tattooed figure approaching was that of Bear – the inmate who had beaten Santiago weeks earlier. Bear got so close to Ramon's face that spittle from his angry mouth fell onto Ramon. "I hear you're running protection for Jose." The quiet Ramon glanced over to see a smiling Jose appraising the action.

Even as a youth, Ramon had never been afraid of confrontation. He recalled a time when three boys from school whose parents were affluent had made fun of his family, calling them "el cerdo," or pigs. He beat the youths so badly that his father had to go to each family to apologize.

Now facing Bear, the still Ramon did not respond verbally. He met Bear's gaze without flinching, as if to communicate that the next move was Bear's. Bear responded with an attempted head butt with his shaved head. The sinewy Ramon, lean and muscular from years of hard work as a farmer, easily avoided the lunge. As Bear's massive body flew by Ramon, he tripped Bear and hit him with a hard left and right punch. Bear was most likely unconscious before he hit the ground. Ramon was quickly surrounded by guards and put in isolation. As he was led away, he heard Jose yell to the others, "I told you, don't mess with Ramon."

Ramon was kept in the "hole" for two weeks. The hole's reputation was actually a misnomer. It was a seclusion cell. Ramon was alone in the cell for twenty-three hours per day. He was let out only one hour a day for exercise, but had no interaction with other inmates.

Ramon actually preferred the hole. The forced isolation allowed him to recall the happier times of his youth. He recalled being a young boy, following his dad as he planted the crops. His father would examine the soil by taking it in his hands and bringing it so close to his nose, he seemed to kiss it. "This is where we will plant the coffee, Ramon. It will grow well here." Ramon grew to love the rich earth surrounding the family farm, where they also grew sugar cane, corn, and tobacco.

Ramon remembered the happy nights, when after a day of hard farm work, the family would gather around the dinner table. Maria and his mother would cook their tasty pupusas. His dad would roll a cigarette from his tobacco, and he and Luis would strum their guitars. Alone with his thoughts, Ramon could almost inhale the wonderful smells of his home.

Invariably, Ramon's happy thoughts were interrupted by the awareness that his family had been destroyed. Since he was a young boy, Ramon had felt responsible for his family. His illiterate father took him, not his older brother Luis, to buy supplies. Ramon had an alert mind and was not afraid to bargain with the suppliers who tried to take advantage of his unschooled father. Once Ramon observed a store clerk intentionally move a decimal point so that tobacco seeds became more costly. The ten-year-old Ramon did not hesitate to correct the clerk on his "error."

As he got older, Ramon saw the dangerous clouds emerging in El Salvador before anyone else. He saw how even his own neighbors – good people once – were caught on either side, for or against the government. All around them, Ramon saw people justifying the use of violence to solve political problems. Ramon wanted nothing more than to work in the rich El Salvadoran soil, but as he watched the violence grow in his homeland, he looked north to America as his family's salvation. Ramon had felt an obligation to save his family. But, in these darkest hours, alone in his cell, Ramon regretted moving to America. "We should have stayed in El Salvador," he whispered to no one.

Ramon was out of seclusion for a week when he was approached again by a fellow inmate. He closed his fist as the older man approached. "You got quite a reputation around here," said the man. Ramon had noticed this man soon after entering Chauncey. He looked different than any of the other inmates, whose skin seemed to resemble the prison's gray walls. The old man's white hair was neatly trimmed, and his skin was suntanned. He seemed to have a special status in the prison, as he had access privileges and bantered easily with the guards. Ramon would later learn from this person that he attributed his healthy image to his Italian heritage, rigorous workouts, and stimulating reading.

The older inmate reached out his hand to Ramon, who kept his fist tight. "My name is Americo Pasquale. My friends call me Army. I thought I would introduce myself, because you and I compose two-thirds of the murderers here." Ramon responded firmly, "I am not a murderer." "Neither am I, kid," replied Army. "I was just stupid thirty years ago, and killed someone for having sex with my wife."

Ramon suspiciously gauged what this man wanted from him, while also taking in his physicality. Army looked more like a banker than an inmate. He projected the regal bearing of the rich politicians in Ramon's native El Salvador. The old man was trim and had intense eyes that appeared to look through the person he was talking to. Ramon examined his unlined face and tried to gauge his age – he could be anywhere between fifty and seventy. Army proceeded to tell Ramon the purpose of his visit. "I've been here longer than any other inmate," he explained. "I'll probably never get out of here. I thought you might like to know how I survived this long – by reading. Books have taken me around the world, even though I never left Vermont."

"You have probably seen that I have some privileges here," Army continued. "I was a lot like you when I first came — angry at the world. I would most likely be dead now if I did not run the library here. The books matured my mind in a way that I learned to forgive myself."

Turning to leave, Army said, "I run the library here. I'm always looking for assistants. It will make your time go faster here if you work around books."

Ramon did not say a word and did not know what to make of the strange encounter. The suspicious Ramon knew that everyone in the prison had an angle. He went back to his cell perplexed that the man did not seem to want anything from him. Yet the idea of working around books was foreign to Ramon. His education had been largely centered on the health of his farm. Ramon's formal education had ended in the eighth grade, because his dad needed help from both of his sons. Even though his reading skills were rudimentary, Ramon had always been a quick learner. But he wasn't even sure he could read a book today.

In the days after his meeting with Army, Ramon continued his isolation from others in angry silence. In fact, part of his agreeing to meet Chelsea that one time was to unleash the anger burrowed within him. "Let the Ryan family become aware of what suffering they have caused," he concluded. He didn't tell Chelsea the full story, because he believed she didn't deserve to know it.

When Maria asked to see him, he refused. He was too ashamed and felt that somehow he had let her down. He was afraid that meeting her would stir up memories which would make his incarceration worse. However, he did accept the Madonna statue from her and hid it with his toiletries, so that other inmates would not see it.

One day on his way to his cafeteria job, Ramon went out of his way to look at the library. Careful that the ever-present Army did not see him, Ramon had to admit that the library was impressive. It consisted of two large rooms with so many books, thought Ramon, that he could not possibly read them all in his twenty-year sentence.

His attempts at evading Army were not successful, however. Those alert blue eyes brought Army to the library door. Ramon would not enter. He hid his embarrassment with defiance. Army told him to wait a moment. He returned with a worn hardcover book entitled "El Salvadoran History". Ramon looked at the ancient text, thinking it had no relevance to him. But he took it from Army, and without a thank you, Ramon carried it to his cell.

Ramon did not pick up the book for three days. Then one afternoon, a bored Ramon slowly opened the book to the first page. He labored, as it took him almost five minutes to read the page. The page revealed that El Salvador was ruled by Spain from the sixteenth through the nineteenth century. Ramon slowly read through the next few pages, and continued reading until three hours later, when he'd finished all of the first chapter. To Roman's surprise, time had passed quickly, and it was already time for dinner.

Roman returned to his cell that night and read two more chapters. He learned that his ancestors fought hard for their freedom from Spain for two centuries, until 1821, when they secured independence. He absorbed how since that time, political and economic upheaval have tormented his country.

As he read, Ramon wrote down words he did not understand. Words like "oligarchy," "conglomerates," and "subsistence farming" filled his notebook. He went to the library the next day and asked Army what they meant. A smiling Army saw that his "fishing" expedition had gone well as he patiently translated their meanings. Soon, Ramon was working at the library every day. He grew to trust his new friend.

Ramon's alert mind quickly adjusted – as if his auto-pilot mental existence had been jolted awake. Ramon initially loved reading about El Salvador – its rich agricultural and cultural history. Army encouraged him to read a book about the 1981 Massacre at El Mozole, where the Salvadoran army slaughtered an entire village of men, women, and children.

Ramon was soon reading up to two books per week. He eventually started reading novels. Army encouraged him to read the classics of Don Quixote and Le Celestina.

Probably because of their connection to death and love, Army and Ramon eventually bonded over the Greek tragedies of Homer, Sophocles, and Aeschylus. Ramon was drawn to the tragic aspects of Greek mythology, as it helped him understand his own rages.

As Ramon and Army slowly formed a friendship over books, Army revealed his own story to his friend. A self-described workaholic, Army had overcome his poor childhood to develop a successful commercial printing business. He had a perfect marriage of ten years with the "most beautiful woman in the world," and had two children—a son, age five, and a daughter, age three. In an instant, his perfect world changed when his wife revealed to him that she wanted to leave him for another man.

She claimed Army was too "self-absorbed" and aloof with her. Ramon listened as Army told him he begged her to stay. They went to marriage counseling and, with some difficulty, he became a better husband. Army thought that the affair was over, but later found out it had never ended.

Ramon could identify with Army's rage. He understood Army's obsession with this man who was taking his wife from him. Army said he confronted the man, but he refused to give up the affair. Several days later, Army flattened the man's tire and watched this man leave his house. As the man changed the flat, Army walked behind him and put a bullet in his head. He then walked into the police station and confessed. He was arrested for the first time in his life. The court determined that Army's premeditated act was worthy of a life sentence without parole. Army's eyes moistened as he said that his wife had left the area, and he had never seen her or his children again.

That night, Ramon returned to his darkened cell and pulled out his favorite quote from Aeschylus: "For the poison of hatred seated near the heart doubles the burden for the one who suffers the disease; he is burdened with his own sorrow and groans on seeing another's happiness." Happy that Maria was safely ensconced in Boston, he had resisted seeing her, until now. He had felt like such a failure. That very night, however, he called his sister Maria and invited her to visit him.

# Chapter 20: Alisa's Anguish

"I WISH YOU HAD NEVER SAID ANYTHING." Try as she might to suppress them, Alisa heard these words again in her head. Safely back in Boston for months, and removed from the violence in El Salvador, she tried not to hear that bitter statement uttered by her drunken father. Unfortunately, her thoughts often returned to violence.

In those first ugly days in San Salvador, as one threat after another confronted the family, Alisa's guilt intensified, and she wanted to tell her family how sorry she was. But every time she tried to talk about it, her mother hushed her. "No, my bebita (baby girl), it's okay", Maria said as she wrapped her thick arms around her daughter. Similarly, it was a taboo subject for Carlos and Roberto.

But to Alisa, this made things only worse. She felt that their regret was on the tip of their tongues, but they needed to protect her. She felt in her soul that her family wished she hadn't said anything about the abuse.

So Alisa retreated into her own world in El Salvador. She slept up to twelve hours a day, and watched television the rest of the time. The funnier the television shows, the better, as they provided her a respite from her guilty conscience. When her mother determined that she and Roberto could go to school, Alisa didn't even care; this from a girl who loved school in America.

Alisa recalled on that first day of school guided by Eduardo, even he sensed something was wrong. "You do not want to go to school, do you?" he asked her. With downcast eyes, Alisa said, "No." "Don't be scared if anyone bothers you. Just let me know," Eduardo told her. "You know, I left school when I was ten," Eduardo boasted. "We learn everything in the streets." Alisa's isolation was just further encouraged by this surreal conversation.

In fact, Alisa eventually did need Eduardo's help at school. School itself was a joke. Nearly seventeen, Alisa was given text books for ten-year-olds. In her eyes, the teachers were just trying to get through the day safely. Students who were obvious gang members came and went from class to class, terrorizing everyone. One classmate was badly beaten in front of Alisa because his parents could not pay "rent."

Alisa surprisingly needed Eduardo's help— not from a boy, but from a girl. This girl was the leader of a female school gang, who was just as scary as the male gangs. They called Alisa "Americano." One day the apparent leader, known as Camila, called her out in class. "You think you are too good for us, Americano?" This was because of Alisa's response that she could not have lunch with Camila and her friends. "I'm sorry, but I have to meet my brother Roberto for lunch." Camila proceeded to slap Alisa in front of the class, and commanded, "You will have lunch with us tomorrow."

The next day Alisa feigned an illness, and Roberto went to school alone. Somehow Eduardo knew something had happened, and he knocked on Alisa's door later in the day. "How come you no go to school today?" Alisa explained about the encounter with Camila. "Come with me." Before Alisa realized it, she was back at her school. Her teacher, Mr. Perez, was just about to leave for the day. Eduardo confronted him. "My friend Alisa is having problems with Camila. I want it to stop." Mr.

Perez did not appear surprised by the demand. "Okay, I'll take care of it."

Alisa returned to school with no more problems from Camila. But Alisa's troubles were not over. She was oblivious to Roberto's growing tensions with another gang. So on the day that a small car pulled up to her outside of school as she waited for her brother, she was unsuspecting. Some boys got out and ordered her to get in. She was squeezed into the compact car, designed for four and filled with six. The car quickly sped away as a bevy of hands roamed all over her body. The driver said, "We are friends of Roberto. We are going to have some fun with you."

Alisa's fear was so great that she later recounted that something snapped within her. It felt like her spirit left her body, and she was watching herself as the boys ripped her shirt off. She could not even feel the hands on her body. At that moment, Alisa thought she was going to die. And she didn't care. Given everything that had happened to her, death would mean no more pain.

Alisa's dreamy peace was interrupted when the car stopped short as it was forced off the road. Suddenly, the menacing face of Eduardo appeared, and he was holding a gun. Soon she was being whisked away by Eduardo's friends in another car. She could not even answer when Eduardo asked her if she was okay. He promised, "Alisa, they will pay for this."

In the days after her abduction, Alisa found herself almost divorced from her feelings. She had been so nervous and on edge about her own family's safety for so long that her nerves seemed to go dormant. The raccoon-like visages of the tattooed boys groping her quickly disappeared. She learned to compartmentalize her feelings to the point that her family remarked how well she was doing. Alisa bought into this tale and told herself she was fine. The only physical evidence that this was not true were her fingernails, bit nearly to the cuticle. That and the bed sheets covered with her sweat when she woke up each morning.

Alisa's new control of her emotions simply did not work beyond bedtime, however. Her dreams inevitably involved scary images of someone or something chasing her. Often, the voices of Jon Ryan or the gang of youths who had abducted her were so loud in her head that they would awaken her. She woke up terrified. But the worst voice she heard was that of her dad, Carlos, saying, "I wish you never said anything!" These words her father had spoken to her before his death haunted her. But she would not tell anyone how much it hurt.

The fortunate turn of legal events for the family helped Alisa to further avoid her feelings. The ink was hardly dry on her mother's visa when Alisa and her family were hustled out of El Salvador and back to America. She soon found herself in a spacious Boston apartment, in which she had her own bedroom for the first time. Unlike Roberto and Maria, who rarely ventured outside, Alisa needed her freedom, and found solitude and comfort walking through the streets of her neighborhood. Soon she entered Boston's English high school as a junior. Her friends from grade school immediately reunited with her as if she had never left.

For Alisa, a busy social life provided the perfect escape from her own mind. It helped that the raven-haired seventeen year old had blossomed into a beautiful young woman. After a few weeks in Boston, El Salvador seemed far, far away.

Alisa was doing so well that she grew irritated with the notion of counseling. To Alisa, it seemed that everyone was telling her something was wrong with her. From school officials to her mother, the need for counseling was constantly brought up. Even Chelsea tried to entice her to go. They did not understand. Alisa just wanted to put it all behind her. She wanted to enjoy her life now. She deserved that.

At school, Alisa completed her academic assignments as tasked. Her passions, however, soon centered on her friends and her social life. Weekends were filled with football games and after-game parties. At one of these parties, her best friend Sonja introduced her to Chris, the quarterback of the football team. To Alisa, this popular, blonde American boy had the cutest dimples she had ever seen.

The foursome—Sonja and her boyfriend Adam, and Alisa and Chris—hung out each weekend. Alisa recalled how the first time Chris leaned in to kiss her, her body froze up. "What's wrong?" asked Chris. Afraid to tell him the real reason, Alisa lied. "I've never kissed anyone before." "You need to relax," said Chris. "Here, let's smoke this." Chris took out a marijuana joint. "This helps me relax after a game." Alisa tried it and loved the feeling it gave her. It felt like her constantly tense body just went limp. "I love it," she said. Chris's kisses then felt as tender as she had hoped.

As time went on, Alisa's social life became much more important than her academic life.

After football season, the two couples went out nearly every night to watch movies or play video games. Weekends, Alisa was often at Sonja's. As her mother's requests to stay home increased, Alisa became frustrated. "Roberto goes to school and work, and you don't say anything to him," she protested. Maria, careful not to upset her daughter, said, "I know Alisa, but I worry about you. You have been through so much." Alisa smiled at her mother. "Trust me, mama. I am okay. I'm just having fun."

Alisa grew to resent any comments by her mother that put limits on her. One day as Alisa was on her way out, Maria stopped her. "Your report card shows your grades have gone down in almost every subject. Even your teachers are worried about you. What's wrong, Alisa?" Alisa finally let out emotions that had been buried for too long. "I'm fine. Leave me alone, Mama. Stop trying to control me," she screamed as she raced past her mother to her awaiting friends.

That night, Alisa was not fine, however. She cried in Chris's arms. She felt so comfortable in his arms that she almost told him about Jon's abuse, about her abduction, about everything. But lying in his strong arms, she realized she could not tell him. How could he still love her if he knew all these things about her?

That same night, when she got home, a marijuana-relaxed Alisa walked right by her mother as she sat watching television on the couch. She felt guilty as she sat down on her bed. Her mother didn't understand her, she thought. No one did. Normally with her marijuana buzz, Alisa was able to go right to sleep. But not tonight. Jon Ryan's handsome but leering face stopped her.

Alisa had not thought about the day of the incident with Jon for a long time. In the past, she had even blamed herself. "I shouldn't have gone into his bedroom." But tonight the image of his penis in her face filled her with rage. "He deserved what happened to him," Alisa told herself. "No one cared what happened to me." She kicked the covers off her and started throwing anything in the bedroom she could get her hands on. Lamps, books, pillows — all went flying against the wall. A scared Maria entered the room, unsure how to help her daughter. Maria quietly watched until Alisa had no energy to throw anything else and slid down to the floor. Maria then folded her exhausted daughter into her arms and repeated over and over, "Mi bebe." Alisa finally whispered, "I'm sorry, Mama. I was thinking of the time with Jon." Maria instinctively understood. She also realized that the time had come for a Ryan to take responsibility for what Jon had done.

# Chapter 21: The Truth

HELENE AND CHELSEA RYAN kept a respectful distance from Maria's family in the months after their return. Alisa, now seventeen, was a junior in high school, and from what Chelsea knew, doing well. Thus she was surprised a year later to receive a call from Maria. Maria informed Chelsea that Alisa's behavior had changed in recent weeks. She seemed angry all the time and did not always come home after school. Alisa's school had called and said she had been truant for several days. She had produced an obviously phony letter signed by her mother to school officials excusing her absences. When the school requested that Alisa see the school counselor, she refused. Maria was worried and asked Chelsea if she would talk to Alisa.

Chelsea had spent considerable time thinking of Alisa and her state of mind. She was amazed that Alisa had functioned as well as she appeared to be at this point. Lots of difficult emotions had to be buried somewhere. Alisa could easily blame herself for all the tragedies that had befallen her family. Her father was dead, and her uncle was in prison, because she'd told her mother what Jon had done. Beyond this, Chelsea could not fathom whether Jon's death also registered in her psyche. For all these reasons, Chelsea had encouraged Alisa to get therapy upon her return from El Salvador. Chelsea had even made an appointment for her with a therapist in a local clinic. Alisa adamantly refused to go.

Chelsea attempted to set up a meeting with Alisa, but Alisa's answer was that her schedule was too busy. Finally, she relented and agreed to go to lunch with Chelsea one Saturday afternoon. The luncheon was polite in nature, Alisa keeping Chelsea abreast of her studies and her infatuation with her favorite musician, Bruno Mars. The day being unreasonably warm, Chelsea suggested they take a ride. They arrived at the playground in Wellesley near Chelsea's old house where they had once played together. Not sure why she even chose this location, Chelsea simply wanted to get Alisa to talk about her feelings.

The two young adults squeezed into children's swings and laughed as they shared memories of their fun times at the park. When she felt it timely, Chelsea revealed that Maria had asked her to speak to Alisa. Chelsea held Alisa's hand and said, "I just want you to get some help. Therapy could help you deal with all the trauma you suffered."

Alisa looked down with tears in her eyes and whispered, "I didn't make it up." Chelsea instinctively knew she was talking about Jon. Alisa continued, "He always seemed to look at me weird whenever I was alone with him. I even told my mother I didn't want to go to your house anymore."

"One day you were at a soccer game, and my mom was cooking in the kitchen. Jon invited me into his bedroom to play video games. I thought it might be okay. As soon as I was inside, he locked the door and wouldn't let me leave. I was so scared, Chelsea, that I couldn't even scream."

As Alisa buried her head in her hands, Chelsea caressed her and whispered, "You don't have to say this." But Alisa raised her head and almost angrily said, "No, I want you to know what your brother did." Chelsea was forced to hear now, even if she didn't want to. Alisa continued, "He stood over me with his back to the door. and pulled his pants down. He forced me to put my mouth on him down there. I started to choke, and he only pushed me harder against him. My body hit the door as he pushed me, and he heard my mother call my name. That was the only reason he let me go. I ran into the bathroom and threw up, Chelsea. You never forget that smell and taste in your mouth. My mother saw stains on my sweater and knew something was wrong."

Chelsea cried as Alisa's forceful voice shared these details. All she could do was repeat, "I'm so sorry, Alisa," over and over. Locking Alisa in her arms, Chelsea sensed that at this moment she somehow, by genetics, represented Jon to Alisa. Chelsea sensed that Alisa was really confronting Jon, and not her.

After a few moments, Alisa's anger subsided. She finally collapsed into Chelsea's arms and murmured, "I know." Demonstrating the complexity of her emotions, Alisa then said to Chelsea, "Everything is my fault. If I had not said anything, my dad would be alive, we would not have been deported, and my uncle would be free."

Now it was Chelsea's turn to be stern. "Look at me," she demanded of Alisa. "This was not your fault – none of it! It is my brother's fault." These words naturally came out of Chelsea's mouth, much to her surprise. It was as if something inside told Chelsea that it was true – Jon had in fact molested Alisa. In admitting this, she felt a strange acceptance that allowed her to freely console Alisa. Chelsea witnessed the illegitimate guilt that Alisa had buried within her and carried for so long.

Alisa agreed to start therapy following this emotional day. During her first therapy session, her therapist explained that unwrapping her emotions was like unraveling a spool of yarn with twisted knots. As you liberated one knot, the next one was tighter and took more effort to unravel. Her therapist honed in on the tremendous guilt that Alisa had displayed with Chelsea.

Over time, Alisa came to accept that she was not responsible for the events which almost destroyed her family. More difficult to unearth was the anger, even rage, at the people responsible for her anguish – Jon, Dr. Ryan, the gangs in El Salvador, and even her dad, for being weak. Eventually she could absorb the love around her – Roberto for agreeing to join a gang, sacrificing his life to protect her; her mom, who fought so hard to shield her, and Chelsea and Helene, who rescued her family.

Chelsea now entered her own therapy free from the denial about Jon that had consumed her. Her mother had continually encouraged this since Jon's death. Therapy helped Chelsea see the signs of Jon's character issues that her family had ignored. It also helped her to forgive her brother as part of the healing process.

Chelsea reached out to her father and asked to meet him for lunch. Dr. Ryan picked her up and took her to their favorite Italian restaurant in the North End of Boston. The restaurant had ten tables packed so tightly that you could reach out and touch your neighbor's delicious handmade raviolis. The husband and wife operators cooked for the continually filled tables as if they were preparing meals at home for their friends. The husband refilled glasses of wine before they were half-empty. The"lobster tail," an Italian desert – a croissant, its shape resembling a large lobster tail, stuffed with rich cream - left all patrons satiated.

The conversation was light as Chelsea and her dad enjoyed their meal. After dinner, Chelsea asked if they could go somewhere to talk. Dr. Ryan agreed, and slowly drove to his favorite Hull Beach spot, where he parked his vehicle as a plane descended overhead. Chelsea told her dad about her recent conversation with Alisa. Dr. Ryan listened but shook his head as Chelsea revealed details of the molestation.

Dr. Ryan insisted that it was not possible for this to have happened. Then in a strange, subconscious argument, he said, "My brother John was not capable of such an act." He caught himself and immediately said, "son." But the idea that he may have overlooked his son's character flaws in an idealization of his brother took hold in his mind. As Chelsea graphically told her dad about the details of Alisa's experience, Dr. Ryan broke down in tears. He was saddened and overwhelmed by what he heard. Earlier, he had admitted to Chelsea his role in deporting Maria and Carlos. "Not a day goes by that I don't regret my participation in that scheme. But I did it for Jon, because he could not have done such things." But even as he spoke, the seed of doubt was planted in his mind.

***

With her therapist's support, Chelsea again reached out to Ramon in prison. In a phone conversation, Chelsea asked that he allow Maria to visit him in Vermont, something that he had previously refused to do. Surprisingly, he now agreed. In fact, he had recently reached out to Maria on that subject.

On the day of the visit, Maria sat alongside Chelsea as she drove the three hours to Vermont. Alisa and Roberto played video games in the back seat. Chelsea considered that they looked like any American family going for a drive. As they drove, Maria talked to Chelsea about Roberto. Things were going better for Roberto. He was earning a small salary as an apprentice plumber. He seemed happy, and was friendly with many of his colleagues. The older plumbers were supportive and told him he had a knack for picking things up quickly. He had also joined a local soccer league. After Maria told Chelsea all this, she smiled, and turned to Roberto saying, "I don't have to worry about you anymore, bicho."

Chelsea listened and observed that she had not heard Maria call her "bicha" since her return. She was now just Chelsea, and she understood why. It was nice to see Maria relaxed today. Since her returnb,Maria had been much more pensive, and her eyes reflected more worry than happiness.

However, today Chelsea saw more joy in those eyes. She observed that Maria had started to put on weight. If I could get her to darken her snow-white hair, thought Chelsea, she would look years younger. At least Maria had allowed Chelsea to have someone trim the long tresses that had accompanied her back from El Salvador. Maria had pulled those white locks tightly into her familiar bun. Chelsea even saw a little of the old Maria as one of those laugh lines crinkled up to her eyes when she shared a joke with Alisa.

The forbidding fortress that housed Ramon lay in front of them. It was as imposing as Chelsea had remembered it. Because of his good behavior Ramon was now allowed person-to-person contact with his visitors. Following security protocol and searches that seemed to terrorize Maria, prison officials led the family to a small room. Keys and clatter soon emanated at the door, and Ramon entered with the beefy guards. One removed Ramon's leg irons, but the wrist locks remained on. One of the guards stayed in the room with them.

While these procedures were happening, Maria almost squirmed with energy. She jumped into Ramon's arms at the first opportunity, and both brother and sister hugged and cried for ten minutes. Alisa and Roberto eventually came to hug

each of Ramon's shoulders. He made pleasant eye contact with Chelsea and mouthed, "Thank you," as the three family members hugged every part of his body.

Ramon had now been in jail for two years, and Chelsea thought he looked like he was at peace with himself. He had put on some weight, and he told them he enjoyed his work as an assistant librarian. "Can you believe I read Shakespeare?" said Ramon. He joked that he was now the most well-read farmer who had left El Salvador. He listened with pride as Roberto discussed welding techniques and Alisa talked about going to college. Maria and he laughed as they recalled the long ride from El Paso to Boston on their first trip to the United States. Little was said that would bring the conversation down. Their parents, Luis, and Carlos had all died with broken hearts and spirits, but that conversation was for another day, thought Chelsea.

Before they knew it, the two-hour visit was over. Ramon pulled Maria close to him and whispered, "I pray to your Madonna every morning." Ramon encouraged more visits, which made his family happy. As they were about to leave, Chelsea asked if she could speak to Ramon alone. The sleepy guard in the corner nodded affirmatively. She asked, "I know I asked this before, Ramon, but did my brother say anything to you that night?" Ramon studied her face closely, and answered, "Yes. Before I fired the second shot, he said, ' I'm sorry'."

The ride home was upbeat for the family. They were happy with Ramon's cheerful demeanor, and his potential with continued good behavior to return to them one day. As Chelsea heard the conversation, her mind was somewhere else. The last words Jon spoke were, to Chelsea, his confession. She knew the repulsive incident was true, but now she also knew that Jon had remorse. If Jon had lived, his remorse would have helped him get therapy for his terrible act. It would have allowed him to use his vast potential to help, rather than hurt someone. Chelsea could be comforted that God had heard those last words and forgiven her brother.

# Chapter 22: Dr. Ryan's Dream

Dr. Ryan drove directly home after dropping Chelsea off after their luncheon date. His new girlfriend called and asked if he wanted company later that night. He declined the offer. He knew he would not be good company tonight. His obsessive mind kept returning to the Freudian slip he'd uttered to Chelsea. Why would he say, "My brother John," when referring to his son?

It led his mind back to his idealization of his brother. While the public may have viewed himself, a physician, as the successful sibling, Dr. Ryan disagreed. His brother John was everything that he wanted to be - popular, a great athlete, and most importantly, beloved by his family. His sisters had adored John. Dr. Ryan had a detached relationship with his sisters. Even now, he barely ever spoke to them. His deceased parents had respected his intelligence, but Dr. Ryan always felt that they viewed him as a little odd.

His closest relationship was with his brother John. John admired and supported him. Dr. Ryan had a hard time believing John when he said, "Jim, you are so smart. I wish it was that easy for me." In those adolescent days, Dr. Ryan told himself he would give up everything to be his brother. He wanted so much to be loved by everyone, like John was.

Dr. Ryan reflected that was why he'd pressured Helene to have another baby. He lied to her. He wanted a son so badly that if Jon had been a girl, he would have as arduously pressured Helene to have another baby, and another, until he had his coveted son. He needed to have a son, a perfect son like his brother John.

As he sat thinking, Dr. Ryan nursed a glass of wine. He thought about the Freudian slip, and suddenly a realization struck him. His glass dropped, the red wine leaving a wave of red on his white rug. As he tried fruitlessly to remove the stain, he started to cry. Maybe this was all about his brother. All that he admired about John, he wanted to remake in his own son Jon. With Jon, he, Dr. Ryan, had a second chance to be handsome, athletic, and popular. He would live this life through his own son.

But, in his effort to recreate himself, had he failed to see the blemishes of his son?

True regret entered Dr. Ryan's mind for the first time. Helene had been right. Jon should have stayed in therapy after the incident with the kitten. Dr. Ryan kept from Helene something his psychiatrist colleague had told him in private. The psychiatrist had warned him that Jon could have a personality disorder. He described it as Narcissistic Personality Disorder (NPD), which involves exaggerated feelings of self-importance, self-admiration, and a disdain and lack of empathy for other people. This type of disdain could lead to abuse of animals or other people.

Dr. Ryan could not stop crying. All the little episodes involving Jon - the girl locked in the closet; his alienation from teammates; his taunting of Roberto - pointed to a troubled nature. Jon, despite the veneer of success, needed help, the type of help his father had failed to get him.

"I should never have listened to that sonofabitch Corcoran," Dr. Ryan repeated to himself over and over. "He's the reason Jon is dead." But as much as Dr. Ryan wanted to believe this, he knew tonight he would have to confront himself, and his own mistakes. Alone in his apartment, he stared at his face in the mirror. No, if Alisa's allegations were investigated, it would have spurred an examination of Jon's behavior. On this night, Dr. Ryan considered the true victim of this Greek tragedy. Chelsea's revelations at dinner about Alisa's abuse were very precise. How could Alisa describe the smell and taste so specifically? Why would she make these comments? Chelsea told him tonight that some semen stains may have been on Alisa's shirt. If he had taken the time to listen to Maria and Alisa, maybe he could have had those stains examined. At least then, there would be no doubt. At least then his troubled son would have gotten the therapy he deserved. Instead, he'd preserved the son he had created and blinded himself to his son's true nature.

Dr. Ryan's night of true honesty had one final piece. A piece he had kept secret all these years. One day, Maria had gone alone to Dr. Ryan with Chelsea's underwear. She stumbled over her words, but blurted out, "I found these in Jon's drawer. It's not the first time. I just wanted you to know this Dr. Ryan." He thanked Maria but never addressed the issue with Jon.

Now Dr. Ryan did something he should have done years ago. He went to his library and pulled out one of his medical books. He looked up Narcissistic Personality Disorder. He viewed a sub-category of the disorder pertaining to an increased risk of sexual abuse. He read, "A narcissist who commits abuse on a child feels powerful because he can control the victim." Everything he read about the disorder seemed to fit his son.

That night, Dr. Ryan tossed and turned, hoping for sleep that would ease his plagued mind. Just before dawn he fell into a deep sleep, he had a vision in that dream. A type of fleeting vision that dreamers have – a vague recollection of the details. But one image was very clear to Dr. Ryan. It was the smiling face of his son. Around his son's arm was the thick arm of an athlete. And there was the equally smiling face of his brother John. So powerful was this visualization that Dr. Ryan immediately woke up with a start. He grabbed his wristwatch – 6 a.m. It was as if he had to touch something tangible, as the smiling faces on the entwined nephew and uncle seemed so real.

Dr. Jim Ryan got out of bed and fell to his knees. Not to pray, but to clean the red wine stain from his rug. He scrubbed and scrubbed until his arm muscles ached. When he was done, only a slight stain still existed. Prone on the floor, Dr. Ryan realized that some stains on one's soul can be cleansed, but not entirely removed. But the important part is the desire to clean it.

Dr. Ryan picked up the phone and called his daughter. An awakened Chelsea whispered, "Everything okay, Dad?" "No, Chelsea. Sorry to waken you. I will need your help to learn to forgive Jon for what he did to Alisa." Chelsea's whole body relaxed. "Of course, Dad, I'll be there for you." Father and daughter then simply cried for what seemed like hours into their respective cell phones.

Dr. Ryan made two more phone calls that morning. Not at 6 a.m., mind you. The receivers of those phone calls would have sworn at him for waking them up. He called his two sisters, and invited them to lunch.

# Epilogue

CHELSEA PUT ON THE FINISHING TOUCHES of eyeliner to accentuate her "baby blues." She turned twenty-eight this year, 2015, and Jon had been dead for seven years. Chelsea wanted to look her best tonight – it was a big night. She gazed at herself in the mirror and liked the person looking back at her. Maybe the old saying is true, she thought — beauty radiates from within. If the interns who constantly asked her out were any sign, Chelsea's physical appearance had matured as well. Her freckles were gone, and she swore her complexion had darkened, close to that of her mother. She even noticed the smallest appearance of laugh lines, similar to Maria's, at the corner of each eye. Given the events of the past ten years, laugh lines were probably a good thing.

"I guess my mother was right," she said to herself with a sarcastic smile. "I won't get married before I'm thirty." But Chelsea's dad had been wrong. She did not become a nurse. No, Chelsea was now a third-year medical resident at Boston University. She was specializing in oncology, and her goal was to become a pediatric physician at Boston's renowned Children's Cancer Center.

Following Jon's death, lots of therapy and soul searching led Chelsea back to her earliest passion – putting smiles on children's faces. She could think of no greater smile that a child could produce as one appreciating that his or her life had been saved. With this goal in mind, Chelsea started taking individual medical courses following Jon's death. She surprised herself with her good grades and received encouragement from her professors. She received a bachelor's degree in biology, which led to medical school exams and acceptance to Boston University Medical School.

The irony of her becoming a doctor was not lost on Chelsea. She was not the child her dad had intended to be the doctor. And conversely, she was not becoming a doctor for some psychological need to supplant Jon. She had always been drawn to the innocence and ego-less warmth of the young, and saving them was, to her, the highest calling.

Chelsea's thoughts were interrupted by her roommate's throaty laugh. "You're going to be late for your own funeral." Chelsea laughed as Lou, her childhood friend, had decided on purple for her hair color tonight. Lou had only two vestiges of her past – weekly changes of hair color, and numerous tattoos, which adorned her arms.

Lou and Chelsea had been roommates for two years, fulfilling a promise they had made to each other as schoolchildren. Like Chelsea, Lou's journey had dragged her to places that some might never recover from. Her parents' divorce had affected Lou deeply. She was lost by high school, and her descent into drugs and sex was the adolescent solution to avoid this pain. By the time she was seventeen, Lou had quit high school, couch surfed with friends, and was using and dealing drugs to survive. She lived lost like this for three years.

By age twenty, Lou looked like she was ten years older. She weighed barely a hundred and five pounds. Recognizing she needed discipline, she joined the Marines. Tested early and often by skeptical male drill instructors, she earned their respect. Her natural athletic ability and toughness stood out. Lou served two tours in Iraq, received numerous commendations, and retired two years ago as a staff sergeant.

While in Iraq, Lou had written a letter apologizing to Chelsea for abandoning her the night she got sick. This had led to a renewal of their tight relationship as youths. On her military leaves, Lou often stayed with Chelsea. When Lou left the military, Chelsea invited her to share her apartment, since they would both be students. Lou was using her military benefits and had enrolled in college to study rehabilitation counseling. She wanted to help the lost souls, of which she was once one.

"I hope you're going to eat tonight, Chelsea," yelled Lou in her strong military voice. Chelsea laughed. Although they were roommates and loved one another, they were as different as night and day. Lou woke up each morning to do one hundred pushups, while Chelsea's idea of exercise was picking up the clothes she left around the apartment. Lou was the neat one, and each night she cleaned the dirty dishes Chelsea left in the sink. Lou's love life was a bit unusual – she dated women as often as men – but both enjoyed her company. Lou had a loud, no-nonsense style. She could easily comment to a chef, for example, that the restaurant food was terrible. But in the manner she said it, even the chef would have to smile.

As usual, take-charge Lou insisted on driving to the restaurant. "The only thing you are good at is saving kids' lives," Lou scoffed. Chelsea smiled, and said, "Don't forget to pick up my mom." The quick reply came back, "Who's the sergeant here?"

Helene looked radiant in her blue sequinned dress. Nearly fifty, she turned the heads of the thirty-something lawyers whenever she entered the courtroom. A district attorney for the last two years, Helene specialized in prosecuting cases involving children. She had a special gift that allowed her to connect with children. They trusted her with their ugly truths, often involving violence, abandonment, and yes, sexual abuse.

Upon graduating law school, Helene had sought placement in the district attorney's office. Corporate law held no appeal for her – she wanted to be an advocate who made a true difference in people's lives. Initially assigned to driving under the influence prosecutions, she had asked to be transferred to the Children's Unit. She did so with her son's memory in mind. Her work often entailed help for the entire family, which was often the root cause of the court's involvement. Chelsea marveled at the irony that it took her brother's death for her own family to heal.

"What an exciting night, ladies," exclaimed Helene, entering the vehicle. Chelsea and Lou groaned as Helene continued with a laugh, "Don't eat too much, or you will lose your figures." Chelsea grinned, thinking that with all the positive changes in her mom's life, this remnant of her past life held firm. Helene was in the midst of her first serious relationship since her divorce. One of those male attorneys admiring her presence in court was on the opposite side of a child guardian case she had worked on. He admired her passion for the family as much as he admired her good looks. Henry Martin, a senior partner in a prestigious Boston firm, was smitten by Helene. Ten years her senior, he wanted to take this relationship further. Helene thought to herself, "If Henry shows up tonight, he might be a keeper."

Chelsea wondered if her father would show up for the grand opening tonight. Since their emotional talks, their relationship had only grown stronger. The impediment that had blocked them – the truth about Jon's death – had been removed. In fact, Dr. Ryan had invited his daughter to a meeting of Parents Forever, a group he had joined. This was a self-help group whose members were united by a sad theme – they were parents who had lost children. Whether they had lost younger or older children, who were victims of homicide, suicide, or cancer, admittance was garnered only by a child's death. Built on the twelve-step program, this club worked because each member knew the pain the others were suffering; a pain someone outside their group would never understand.

Dr. Ryan had been attending the group for the past year. The fifteen-person group had welcomed Chelsea as a guest. As usual, the meeting began with asking if anyone had a special need to share that night. Chelsea's dad raised his hand and said, "I'm proud to introduce my daughter Chelsea. She is going to be a physician, an occupation that I'm sorry to say I never encouraged. More importantly, she helped me to accept the truth about my son. The truth that my beautiful son was capable of doing something very bad. And she helped me to forgive him and myself. Some of you know I lost my son, but until now, I was never able to share the full story."

"I killed my son." For a full hour, Dr. Ryan proceeded to tell the stunned group all of the circumstances behind Jon's death. He relayed step-by-step the tragedy that began with Alisa's allegations, and his denial of them. He admitted to his role in the Gomez family's deportation to El Salvador, and the violence they endured there. He revealed that he unwittingly endangered Maria's family again in El Salvador, when he stopped the $300 stipend to her family after Jon was murdered.

He accepted his role in the death of Maria's husband Carlos, as well as ultimately the death of his own son. Slowly shaking his head he conceded, "I blame myself more than Ramon for Jon's death."

Dr. Ryan continued, "With the help of this group, and my daughter, I am learning to forgive myself." Various group members hugged Dr. Ryan. Many shared similar feelings of guilt and responsibility for their loved ones' deaths. Chelsea was uplifted, and felt that this group gave its members hope for the future.

"We are here," said Lou in her forceful military voice, snapping Chelsea's mind to the present. Bright red lights greeted the women as they exited the car. Chelsea smiled as she read the words on the sign: "Pupusas – Filled with Love." Yes, this was the grand opening of Maria and Alisa's new restaurant. Mother and daughter were beaming as they welcomed new and old friends. Chelsea thought she had not seen Maria this happy since the days when Chelsea had watched her prepare pupusas in her parents' kitchen. Alisa, too, had become expert at folding the pupusas as well as her mother. More importantly, Alisa loved to see the content faces of her customers devouring the mouthwatering treasures.

Two of these smiling faces were those of Max Roosevelt and Elena Sanchez, now partners in and out of their office. Gone was Max's unruly mustache. Elena had set one condition on their personal partnership – remove that ugly thing. This was a no-brainer bargain for a happy Max.

Seated with them was a relaxed Roberto with his arm around a young redhead. She was the daughter of his Irish boss, Ed Murphy. The young couple was already talking marriage. Mr. Murphy could not have been happier. He was impressed by his hardworking and respectful apprentice plumber.

Also seated at the table was a handsome engineering student named Lucca Santos. A native of Brazil, Lucca was in America on an education visa. He was about to graduate with a mechanical engineering degree from M.I.T. One day he hoped to design affordable housing for the many impoverished people in his country.

Lucca had intended to return to his home of San Paulo upon graduation. However, that plan had changed when he started dating Alisa three months ago. He was admittedly prejudiced until then that Brazil had the prettiest women in the world – until he met the radiant Alisa. Thank heaven he was graduating soon, he had often told himself in those three months, since engineering quickly took a backseat to being with Alisa. He was that thunderstruck.

The couple's relationship was further complicated because Alisa was attending culinary school. But they found time to share their deepest secrets with one another. For Lucca, Alisa's revelations about her sexual abuse incidents only increased his admiration of her. Lucca saw that Alisa was as beautiful inside as she was on the outside. Just then, Alisa poked her head out of her new kitchen and blew Lucca a kiss. Lucca turned to Max and asked, "Do you think you can get me a residency visa when I graduate from college?"

At an adjacent table sat Maria's old boss in El Salvador, Nina. Maria had encouraged her friend to visit to help ease her sadness. Yes, her son Eduardo had succumbed to the senseless gang violence of her country. A bullet had pierced his heart in a drive-by shooting near his mother's restaurant. Nina's only relief was that her handsome son had not been mutilated. She was able to kiss her son, laid out in his casket, one last time. Maria hoped to convince her friend to stay in the U.S. permanently.

The violent tentacles of San Salvador had captured another victim. Mario Ramirez would not be its drug czar. He had simply vanished. Rumor on the street was that he disappeared the night he was to attend a meeting of all the gangs with the government officials. A government spokesman said that he moved to Honduras. Ramirez's rival, Hector, now collected all the rents at the Market every Saturday.

Also present was Rocky Conley and his wife, Nancy. After his sudden retirement, Rocky had opened a law office in Vermont. He tired very quickly of representing defendants that he had formerly put in jail.

To Nancy's credit, she did not object when Rocky's old hometown of Everett, Massachusetts, recruited him to coach their renowned football team. However, unknown to Nancy, Rocky had actually put out feelers to see if his old team was interested in such a reunion. He was thrilled to be coaching young men in the sport he loved. In his first year as coach, his Everett Crimson Tides won the State Championship.

Rocky had kept up a relationship with the reformed Ramon, who was still in prison. From that relationship, Rocky had met with

Maria in Boston. He soon loved her pupusas almost as much as his Everett meatballs.

In a final bit of justice, Rocky had helped authorities to examine Ed Corcoran's behavior in the Ryan case. As a result, Edward Corcoran had lost his private investigator's license. However, something told Rocky that this was not the end of Corcoran's devious acts.

Chelsea was unsure if her father would come tonight. Part of his unease had centered on Maria's and Alisa's feelings toward him. Although he had called Ramon in prison, and each had forgiven the other, his guilt about mother and daughter was worse. Just then, Chelsea saw her dad coming through the door. Before even Chelsea could greet him, Maria had her arms around Dr. Ryan. Each soon collapsed into each other's arms. Soon Alisa joined the hugfest – the three entwined in tears. But they were tears of forgiveness and strength. The pupusas had fulfilled their destiny of love!

Two hundred miles away, Ramon was contently reading, to his own surprise, David Copperfield. Ramon has begun the day as usual, on his knees praying to the Madonna. He always asked for forgiveness for killing the young boy. He could never say Jon's name. He prayed that God would have mercy on him and heal the boy's heart. For in his darkened cell, Ramon often remembered those last

moments with the "boy." What he had never told anyone, not even Maria or Chelsea, was that he had second thoughts on those lonely nights he spent in the Vermont woods planning the murder. One night, he went to the campus and saw Jon practicing basketball with his teammates. Jon's exuberant play convinced Ramon this young boy had a life ahead of him that could be changed. Leaving the gym that night, Ramon loitered a bit and happened to see Jon walking to his dorm with a young woman. Unexpectedly, Jon suddenly slapped the face of his companion. In anger Ramon said to himself, "He is not a good person!"

The night of the murder Ramon was again ambivalent about acting on his revenge. He then surprised even himself when he shot Jon in the leg. Ramon, in a dreamlike state, heard Jon's screams and was uncertain about firing again. In broken English he stammered, "Why you hit the girl?" Jon, clutching his bloody leg, uttered, "The bitch deserved it." The last word was barely out of the boy's mouth when Ramon placed the gun behind Jon's head and fired.

Ramon prayed to the plastic Madonna that Jon's first words upon facing God were, "I'm sorry." Then he returned to his book, which took him to freedom from the walls around him.

# ABOUT THE AUTHOR

Stephen Rocco is a third-generation funeral director in a funeral home outside of Boston. In addition to working as a funeral director over 40 years, he was a family mediator. He was an instructor at Mt Ida College for many years and Co -Director of its National Center For Death Education. Stephen and his wife, Lidia, have been blessed with four children and three grandchildren (and hopefully many more).

www.ingramcontent.com/pod-product-compliance
Lightning Source LLC
Chambersburg PA
CBHW032211030726
47494CB00020B/951